MW01146800

Married

Married Series Book 5

Victorine E. Lieske

Published by: Victorine E. Lieske

SCOTTSBLUFF, NEBRASKA

Victorine E. Lieske
PO Box 493
Scottsbluff, NE 69363
www.victorinelieske.com

Publisher's Note: This is a work of fiction. Names, characters, places, and incidents are a product of the author's imagination. Locales and public names are sometimes used for atmospheric purposes. Any resemblance to actual people, living or dead, or to businesses, companies, events, institutions, or locales is completely coincidental.

Book Layout © 2017 BookDesignTemplates.com

Acting Married/ Victorine E. Lieske. -- 1st ed.
ISBN 978-1548491833

This book is dedicated to all my lovely alpha and beta readers who have helped me polish up this story! Lea Carter, Audrey Rich, Jean Newman, Debra Erfert, Mary Gray, Amy Linnabary, Julie Spencer, Brookie Cowles, Carol Anne Olsen Malone, Crystal Walton, Melanie Snitker, Rachel John, Kris Noorman, Sabrina Sumsion, Dee Feeken Schmidt, Mary Unger, C.K. Volnek, Kathryn Gilmore, and G.M. Barlean. You are all awesome! And a special thank you to my editor, Hayley Brooks. You make me look good! And of course, to my dear husband, who puts up with my writing obsession. I love you, honey.

Chapter 1

*T*ara grabbed the scrubber brush, bucket, and spray bottle, then climbed into the large shower. It was made of some fancy tile, Italian maybe, with an intricate pattern carved into it. The shower alone probably cost more than a year of her apartment rent. *What a waste.* She sighed and started spraying.

She'd been at this job for three days and hadn't even seen the owner of the house yet. Party boy Rick Shade must be off at a film shoot somewhere. She really didn't care. As long as he paid her on time, she'd clean up after him. In fact, she preferred not to see him.

Rick was known for his crazy escapades. Like most actors, he didn't have a stable life. But he sure had money. His mansion was bigger than

Jack Sparrow's ego, all for one self-absorbed actor.

She almost didn't take the job, but being stuck in L.A. and newly divorced, she couldn't afford to be picky. And since her skills consisted of making peanut butter and jelly sandwiches and buckling in booster seats, she didn't exactly qualify for much.

Oh well. She'd rather clean Rick Shade's toilets than be homeless. She'd do anything to protect Kylee from living on the streets. It wasn't like she could go back home, and no four-year-old should have to worry about where she'd sleep next.

Ugh. She forgot to fill the bucket at the sink. And she'd sprayed cleaner all over the door handle. She didn't really want to touch it. Maybe if she held the bucket up to the showerhead, she could fill it that way. She grabbed the handle and lifted it up, then turned on the shower.

Freezing water came at her from the sides of the shower, and she yelped. She instinctively lowered the bucket and more water showered down on top of her. "Snap!" she yelled as water sprayed in her eyes and ran down her back. Dang, it was cold! She tried to find the lever to turn it off while hopping from one foot to the other in a lame attempt to avoid getting wet.

"That's an interesting way to clean a shower," a deep voice said.

Tara found the handle and cranked it, shutting off the water. She turned to find Rick standing on the other side of the glass. Heat rose to her cheeks as water dripped from the tendrils of hair that had escaped her bun, her now-wet uniform sticking to her body. She shoved the bucket in front of her so Rick wouldn't get a better view than she wanted. "Sorry," she said, unsure of what else to do.

He chuckled, his smile making her breath catch. He opened the shower door and motioned for her to exit. His sandy-blonde hair was styled to look like he'd just gotten out of bed. It was the sexy mussed-up look. He was wearing a t-shirt that accentuated his muscular build, and jeans that hugged him just right. The term "movie star" didn't do him justice. And she just stood there, staring like an idiot.

"You can come out. I really don't think you meant to take a shower with your clothes on."

She shook her head, stepping onto the mat. "No." She looked at the bucket as if that explained everything.

He held out his hand and she stared at it, not comprehending what he wanted.

"Give it to me. I'll fill it. You can dry off with a towel." He motioned to the cabinet.

Great. Now she looked like an even bigger idiot. She handed him the bucket and grabbed a towel. Rick walked over to the tub and stuck the bucket under the faucet. "You're new here."

She nodded, her heart pounding so fast that she was unable to string together a few simple words to form a sentence.

He finished at the tub and gave her the handle. "You're doing great," he said as he left, a smile in his voice.

Perfect. Just how she wanted the day to go. She patted her hair with the towel, wondering how many more ways she could find to look like a moron in front of Rick Shade.

***

Tara arrived at work the next day, determined to blend into the background. She was the maid; she needed to do her job and not draw attention to herself. If she didn't mess up, maybe she could earn enough to pay off all the legal fees she'd accrued. Bobby had dragged things out in court, and now she owed way more than the child support checks he was forced to send would cover. He was a class-act jerk. Too bad she hadn't seen that side of him until after they'd married. Or maybe his sudden fame made him that way. She probably would never know for sure.

Greta, who was in charge of the staff, waved her over. She was a thin woman with an eye for details, who managed the staff with precision. "We're short on kitchen staff today. I'll need you to start there."

"Okay." Tara walked down the hall to the kitchen.

She walked in and almost gasped. State-of-the-art everything. Three ovens. Two stovetops. Marble counters that wrapped around three sides of the room with an island in the middle. Eliza, the head chef, smiled in relief when she entered. "Good. You're here. Take this into the parlor." She shoved a tray into Tara's hands. "The one on the left is for Rick. I've got to get these cream puffs out of the oven or they'll burn."

Tara peered down at the two coffee mugs. "Where is the parlor?" She'd mostly spent the week cleaning the rooms upstairs.

"First room off the front entrance. You'd better hurry. Rick doesn't like to wait." Eliza shooed her out the door.

5

Perfect. She picked the direction that made the most sense and started down the hallway. She passed by a dining hall, a library, and a room with a bunch of swords on the walls before she heard male voices.

As she neared, she couldn't help but overhear them.

"I don't care what anybody says. I'm not going to spend one minute alone in a room with that harpy, much less announce an engagement." The smooth voice was unmistakable. Rick.

Another male voice answered. "They're giving the part to Zac Efron because of this last stunt you pulled. The story was front-page news."

Tara slowed. She wasn't exactly eavesdropping. She was just making sure the coffee didn't spill on the tray.

"No one reads the tabloids."

"The *L.A. Times* is not a tabloid." The sound of a newspaper slapping onto a table carried out into the hall.

Tara entered the room. Rick was sitting in a wingback leather chair, draped over it like it was the most comfortable place he could be. She tried to not look at him. He had a way of sucking all the air out of her lungs. And he was even more gorgeous today. Dang, she was looking.

His gaze connected with hers and he winked. Heat crept up her neck. Busted. She stepped further into the room and couldn't help but notice the newspaper headline on the coffee table. *Rick Shade caught skinny dipping.* The article included a blurry photo.

A snort came out of her before she had the chance to pull herself together. Both men stared at her, and she sobered. "Excuse me," she said.

Rick's lips twitched.

She set the tray down on the server against the wall. Super. She'd messed up again. If her training had drilled anything into her head, it was that she was supposed to be invisible and never speak unless spoken to. Why couldn't she do a simple job? She needed to give them the coffee and get out of there.

"Phil, I know you're talking as my manager, but I'm not marrying Vikki Castle. Not even if it saves my career. Have you spent any time with her? She's horrible. All she talks about is her hair and how many pairs of shoes she has."

Did movie stars really marry who they thought would boost their career? She mentally chastised herself for not concentrating on her job. She looked down at the cups. Which one was she supposed to give Rick? Left or right? A bead of sweat broke out on her forehead.

"You wouldn't have to stay married for long. Maybe a year. Showing the public you're in a committed relationship would be good."

Tara picked up the mugs and turned toward Rick. She had a fifty-fifty chance to get it right. She walked toward him.

He smirked. "I'd rather marry her." He pointed at Tara.

Startled, she tripped over her own feet and coffee spilled on Rick's lap. He jumped up from the chair and took the mugs from her.

"Oh! I'm sorry!" She grabbed a napkin from the accent table and started dabbing at the coffee before realizing that probably wasn't the most appropriate thing she could do. She slowly backed up, twisting the napkin in her hands. "Sorry," she said again.

"Marry the maid?" Phil laughed, ignoring the spill. "That could actually bring you great press."

Rick stared at her, one eyebrow raised, his intense gaze penetrating through her.

Crud. She was so fired. Worse than fired. He'd probably charge her for ruining his million-dollar jeans. She'd walk away from this job owing him money.

Phil stood and came toward her. "She has pretty eyes."

Rick set the coffee mugs down on the table and nodded. "We could do something else with her hair."

Her hand flew to her bun. What was wrong with her hair? And why were they talking like she wasn't even in the room?

"She has a nice hometown look," Phil said. "The everyday housewife will love that."

Housewife? Were these guys insane? Tara bit her cheek to stop herself from giving them a piece of her mind.

Rick walked around her like she was a quarter horse he was thinking about buying. "This could make national news." He finally spoke to her. "You're Tara, right?"

Wait, Rick knew her name? The situation was too ludicrous to be believable. Her gaze bounced between the two men. "You're a few clowns short of a circus. I'm being punked, right? Where's the camera?"

"Her Midwestern accent is quite endearing," Phil said.

Rick's lips curled up in a small smile. "It is." He focused on her. His gaze flitted to her hands. "Are you single?"

Surely they weren't serious about her marrying Rick Shade. That was crazy, and she had to bite her tongue to not tell them both off. She needed this job. "Yes, but you don't want me to be a part of your publicity stunt. I have a four-year-old daughter."

Phil clapped his hands together. "That's great! We can get the kid in the photos. The public will eat it up. Every single mother out there will be swooning."

Rick frowned. "I don't know. A kid would complicate things."

Finally someone was seeing reason. She nodded enthusiastically. "Yes, a big complication. So, you see, it would never work."

"The daughter would touch the hearts of America," Phil said. "Trust me."

Rick shook his head. "No. I don't want to do it if there's a kid involved." He sat back down on his chair and wiped at his jeans where she'd spilled the coffee. "It was an interesting idea, but it won't work."

Phil got a desperate look in his eye. "It will work! It has to. You need to do this."

Tara blurted out, "I agree with Rick." They ignored her.

Rick scowled at Phil. "I said no." He turned his gaze on Tara. "It won't work."

She nodded at him and left the room. What had happened to everyone? They were crazy. Thank heavens Rick wasn't insisting on marrying her. That would have been a nightmare.

Chapter 2

wo weeks later, the call came that Rick hadn't gotten the lead role in the live-action remake of *Aladdin*. He was counting on that role. The bitter taste of failure filled his mouth. "What did they say?" he asked, gripping his cell phone, and pacing his office.

Phil sighed. "They liked your audition, but didn't think you were the right fit, which basically means your reputation killed the deal."

"What?"

"I'm telling you, you've got to stop going out and partying every night. No one wants to hire someone unstable."

Rick cursed under his breath. He needed this. It had been months since he had any kind of job. He had money, but he wasn't ready to become a has-been. He needed to stay in the public eye. Acting was his passion. His true love. It was all he had left after—

He stopped short. He didn't want to think about Scarlett. "All right, all right. What if I married the maid? Would that help me get the part?"

Phil was silent for a few seconds. "I think it's a good idea, but only if you start acting like a married man."

Keep a low profile for a while? He could handle that. "Okay."

"That means you've got to give up the booze."

Rick stopped, heat rising to his face. "Why? I'm not a drunk."

"Prove it. Become a family man. Clean up your act. They don't want to hire some party boy."

Rick ran a hand through his hair and exhaled. Party boy. Sure, he'd made some mistakes, but he wasn't really like that. Admittedly, he hadn't done much to contradict his bad reputation.

He needed this publicity stunt. Barely thirty and his career was sliding down the toilet. "Fine." He'd stay home and become boring.

"Go talk to the maid. Pay her whatever you can to convince her to marry you for a year. Then after that you can get a quiet divorce. Maybe we can say she cheated on you. Play the sympathy card."

"Good idea. Okay. I'll get her to agree to it."
Women usually responded well to him when he
turned on the charm. It shouldn't be too hard.

Rick hung up the phone and stalked down the
hallway toward Greta's office, where he found
her behind the desk. He folded his arms and
cracked a smile. "Where's the new girl?"

Greta lifted an eyebrow. "Tara?"

"Yes."

"She's in the second guest bathroom."

He pointed at her and grinned. "Perfect. Oh,
and could you have Carter pull the car around
front and wait for me there?"

"Sure."

"Great, thanks."

He took the stairs two at a time and turned
down the hall toward the guest bedrooms. He
wasn't in love with the idea of marrying for publicity, but he was desperate; and besides, people
got married for stupid reasons all the time. It
wasn't like he was committing his life to her. It
was just a year. He'd do it to get the next big part.
It had the potential to put life back into his career.

All his guest bedrooms were large, with their
own attached bathrooms. He hadn't spared any
expense. The bathroom was equipped with a Ja-
cuzzi, a shower, built-in cabinets, and a floor-

length mirror. He found Tara bent over, scrubbing the toilet. "Hey," he said, rocking back on his heels.

She swiveled around. "Oh! You scared me." She stood there, her hand on her heart, the other holding a dripping scrub brush. Her black and white uniform hugged her curves, and he took a second to admire them.

Her dark hair was pulled up into that silly bun again, but several tendrils had escaped, coming down to frame her face. She was definitely pretty, and perhaps a bit younger than he'd originally suspected. Maybe mid-twenties. Her skin was smooth, and he wondered what it would feel like to touch it. She'd tug at America's hearts.

"Do you need me to work on another room, sir?" Her gaze was skittish, bouncing around but never really settling on him.

"No. I'd like to talk to you."

She frowned, which made her look even more appealing for some reason. "Am I fired?"

He chuckled. "No, don't worry. It's nothing like that." He walked toward her and took the scrub brush from her hand. "I just want to talk."

She nodded, still not looking at him. "Okay, sir."

Man, she was uptight. She needed to relax. "You don't have to call me 'sir.'" He tossed the brush into the bin and put his arm around her. She stiffened, and he tried not to pay attention. "Let's go eat lunch."

She hesitated. "I don't think..."

"Don't think. Just come with me." He gave her his best sexy grin and herded her out of the guest bathroom. If he laid it on thick enough, she'd be putty in his hands.

She stopped. "I've been cleaning toilets."

"Then wash up." He waved to the bathroom. "I'll wait for you."

Her frown deepened, but she did as he said. Then he ushered her through the house and out the front where the driver had the limo waiting. Carter opened the door and motioned for her to go in. She hesitated a moment, then slid in. He climbed in after her.

Going out in public with her would be good. He could get some photos of them together with her in her uniform and get some publicity that way. Start the rumor mill going.

"Where would you like to go, sir?" Carter asked.

Rick put his arm on the back of the seat. "Café Med." There was sure to be paparazzi hanging around.

Tara sat twisting her hands together, back stiff, so he decided to put her at ease. "How do you like working for Greta? Has she been nice to you?"

"She's been fine." Tara didn't look at him.

"Have you enjoyed working at the house?"

Finally, she turned to him, but he didn't expect the flat look. "Are you asking me if I *enjoy* cleaning your bathrooms?" Her eyes grew wide and she clamped her hand over her mouth. "Sorry," she said under her hand. "I didn't mean that."

Rick found himself laughing, which surprised him. Women rarely made him truly laugh. "Yes, you did."

"I'm sorry. My mouth sometimes gets me into trouble. I love my job and really want to keep it." She stared down at her hands again, which went back to twisting and wringing.

"I'm not going to fire you. In fact, I want to give you a raise."

She didn't look at him.

He tried again. "And you wouldn't have to clean anymore." He leaned closer to her, giving her his best Hollywood grin.

"I don't want to marry you," she blurted.

18

"Ouch." He removed his arm from behind her on the seat.

She turned her gaze to him. "I don't mean to hurt your feelings, but I don't want to be a part of your publicity stunt. I have a daughter—"

"I know." And he wasn't too thrilled about it either. But he was kind of stuck. "It'll be fine. All she'll need to do is pose for a few photo shoots. The rest of the time, we can keep her out of the media's eye."

Tara swallowed, her face draining of color. "I'm sorry. I just don't think it's a good idea."

What was wrong with her? There were a million girls out there who would die to be seen with him in public. He met dozens each night. Why was this one being so stubborn? He decided to change tactics. "I can make it financially worth your while."

She paused, and he thought maybe he'd hit on something, so he continued. "I'm willing to pay you for your time."

She bit her lip and shook her head. "No, I can't—"

"A hundred thousand dollars," he blurted, before he had the chance to think about it.

Her eyes grew wide and she went very still. "What?" she whispered.

19

He hadn't meant to say that much, but for some reason getting her to say yes had become a challenge, and he never backed down from a challenge. He was not used to losing. "A hundred thousand. And all you have to do is marry me."

Her gaze lifted to his, and he was stunned by the beauty in her dark brown eyes. "What happens if you don't get the part?"

"If you've fulfilled your end of the bargain, you'll still get the hundred thousand."

She took in a deep breath and let it out slowly. He could see the war going on behind her eyes. Just when he thought she was going to say yes, she shook her head.

"Stop." He held up a hand. "Don't answer yet. Let's eat lunch, and you can think about it." The car turned onto Sunset Boulevard. They'd be there in a minute.

"Okay."

When they arrived, he got out of the car and took her hand to help her onto the sidewalk. As he suspected, paparazzi lined the walk and cameras flashed. Tara shielded her face. "It's okay," he said in her ear, as he put his arm around her. "Just ignore them."

He paused to give them a smile he knew would be in all the tabloids, and then he rushed her inside. The server seated them, took their drink orders, and then left them to look over the menu.

Tara fidgeted. "What do you suggest?"

"I like the Linguine Alle Vongole, if you're looking for something light. The Filetto Al Barolo is good if you like filet mignon."

"I'll have the linguine." She folded her menu and placed her hands in her lap.

He leaned back in his chair and took a good look at her. She was nervous. But something else lay beneath the surface, and he couldn't quite peg it. "Where are you from?"

"Iowa."

He raised an eyebrow. "What brought you to L.A.?"

She frowned. "My ex-husband."

Oops. Maybe that wasn't the best question to ask. "What are your plans for the future?"

"Right now I just want to pay off all the legal fees from the divorce. After that, I'd love to move back to Iowa. Raise my daughter in the Midwest where they have good values." Her cheeks colored. "I mean . . . no offense."

He laughed. "None taken. So, doing this with me could help you reach that goal, right?"

"Right. And that's the only reason why I'm considering it." She cringed. "Again, no offense."

He picked up his water and sobered. This girl wasn't into him at all, which was frustrating. He was used to being able to get what he wanted from women. "I'm beginning to take offense."

She didn't look him in the eye. "I just want to live a quiet life. I'm all done with the limelight."

He squinted at her. "What do you mean?"

"My ex is Bobby Goodwin."

"The unknown who landed the big role in the last James Bond movie? He's the one that..." He stopped when he realized who she was. "Oh." He remembered the story now. Bobby had made it to the big screen and tossed his wife and kid by the wayside for some supermodel.

The pain was evident in her eyes. He scrubbed a hand over his face, and empathy bubbled up inside him. It was obvious Bobby had hurt her badly. "Sorry," he said, his sentiment somehow inadequate.

She lifted one shoulder and let it fall. "It happened. I can't change it." Her gaze turned to meet his. "But I can protect myself from anything like that happening again."

Rick swallowed, unsure of what to say. "This would be different."

"Yes, it would," she whispered.

The server came back and took their order. After she left, he tried again. "Will a hundred thousand pay off your debt and allow you to move to Iowa?"

Tara stared at the table and shifted in her seat. "Yes."

"Good." He smiled, tipped his glass toward her, and took a sip of his water. "Then I see only one logical course of action."

"If I agree to this, what will be expected of me?"

She was going to say yes, he was sure. He grinned. "I'd have my attorney write up a contract. You'd be expected to be seen with me as we announce our engagement. We'd have a few public appearances, at least one with your daughter. Then we'd get married with the media covering the wedding. After that, we'd be seen on a honeymoon, and then a few more appearances. We'd stay married for one year, then get a quiet divorce."

She eyed him. "And in private?"

He shot her a frown. "This would only be a marriage on paper. You would not have any obligations when we were in private. What did you think I was proposing?"

She folded her arms and cocked one eyebrow at his question. "All I know of you is what I've read in the papers, and let's just say that hasn't been favorable."

She was right. He'd helped perpetuate his own bad reputation on purpose, and had gone too far. Now he needed to rein it in. "Don't believe everything you read in the papers."

"I don't."

He studied her, back straight, fingers gripping the table like a lifeline. What did she think he was? Some kind of psycho? "So, you'll do it?"

"Who will take care of Kylee while we're out in public?"

"I can hire a nanny."

She didn't look like that pleased her, but she nodded. "Okay."

"Is that a yes?" He hated to admit it, but he was holding his breath, waiting for her to answer.

"If I say no, will I be fired?"

He leaned back and exhaled, frustrated. "Of course not. I'm not trying to strong-arm you into anything. I just see this as a mutually beneficial arrangement. If you don't want to do it, then fine."

A scrutinizing look came over her and she slowly nodded. "Alright, then."

Rick wanted to scream. "You'll marry me?"

She looked away from him, as if she couldn't bear to gaze on him anymore. "Yes."

Finally, she said yes. He should have felt happy, getting what he wanted, but for some reason the triumph wasn't what he expected. The victory had fallen flat.

Chapter 3

ara sat across the desk from Rick's attorney, signing papers. Mountains and mountains of papers. Sweat broke out on her forehead as she agreed never to breathe a word of the setup to anyone. She signed that she would not be entitled to more money than agreed upon, that she would not be able to sue, take unauthorized photos, or countless other things a person could think of, and some things she never would have thought of.

When the signing was done, she exited the office feeling stripped and exposed. Why was she doing this? She couldn't help but feel like it was a stupid mistake she'd regret the rest of her life. She walked through the marble hallways and up the stairs toward her new place of residence. Rick's master guest bedroom.

As she entered the room, Kylee cried out in delight. "Mommy!" She ran toward her, little pigtails bobbing, and hugged her legs.

Sophie, the older woman from her apartment complex who had been watching her daughter, set down a black garbage bag full of Kylee's clothes. Sophie looked around the room. "Are you sure you know what you're doing?"

Tara shook her head. "No, but do we ever know when it comes to matters of the heart?" She'd told Sophie she was moving in with Rick, and nothing more.

Kylee squealed and climbed on the king-sized monstrosity. "Is this my bed?"

"No, you'll have your own room," a low voice said behind her.

Tara turned to see Rick in the doorway. Why did her heart always pound when he was near? She tried to steady her breathing. He was just a man. A smokin' hot man, but still. She wanted to argue with him about where Kylee would sleep, but with Sophie there, she just forced a smile.

Sophie frowned and backed up. "Well, I best be going."

Tara put her hand on Sophie's arm. "Thank you for bringing Kylee. I appreciate all you've done."

Sophie cast a shadowed look at Rick before nodding. "You're welcome." She left the room.

Kylee climbed down from the bed and walked up to Rick, her head tilted back as she looked up at him. "Who are you?"

"I'm Rick."

Tara grabbed her daughter's hand, pulling her away from him. Rick had said he wasn't fond of children, and she didn't want Kylee to bother him. "Kylee, are you hungry for lunch yet?"

Her daughter's big, brown eyes stared at her. "Sophie gave me fish crackers."

"That's fine. Let's go see what else there is to eat."

"I'll have the kitchen make some lunch." Rick pulled his cell phone out of his pocket.

Tara held up her hand. "No, that's okay. We can go make ourselves something." It was stupid to sit around and wait while the staff made her a sandwich. This morning she *was* the staff. She was capable of putting peanut butter on bread.

Holding Kylee's hand, she led her down the stairs and through the hallways to the kitchen. She'd gotten used to the layout of the house and could maneuver her way around for the most part.

When she entered the kitchen, she waved to Eliza. "We're just going to make a peanut butter and jelly sandwich." Tara opened the cupboard and pulled out a loaf of bread.

Eliza frowned. "I was just fixing lunch."

"It's okay. I don't mind making a sandwich for my daughter."

Eliza put her hand on her hip. "Rick called down and asked that I do it."

Tara froze. She watched as Eliza pulled the peanut butter from the cupboard, Tara's blood boiling. Why would Rick do that? She didn't want his staff waiting on her. And she'd told him she wanted to do it. "Could you watch Kylee for a moment?"

"Sure." Eliza sat down on a stool next to Kylee and started spreading the peanut butter.

Tara went to find Rick. If he thought he was going to push his rich-person lifestyle on her, she'd have to set him straight. She found him sitting in his office chair, typing on his computer. He looked up when she entered the room. "Hi."

She narrowed her eyes at him. "Why did you do that?"

He pushed his chair back. "What did I do?"

"You told the staff to make Kylee a sandwich."

"So?"

"I said I would do it."

He stood and came around the desk. "You're going to be married to me soon. You can let the staff do things like that."

She fought the urge to stuff her fist into his pretty face. "I thought this whole thing was to show the public how down-to-earth you are. How you can mingle with the simple people."

He seemed taken aback. "You think I'm a snob?"

"I think you're out of touch with reality. You have no concept of how people live. You've lived in privilege so long you don't even know what it's like to make your own sandwich." She turned to leave, but he grabbed her arm.

"Wait."

She faced him, ignoring the tingling sensation of his skin on hers, and stared down at his hand until he let go.

"I'm sorry. I didn't mean to offend. Most people..." He stopped and chuckled, taking a step back to sit on the edge of his desk. "Well, most people aren't like you."

What did that mean? "You're right. I don't want to be waited on, hand and foot."

He held up his hands in a surrender motion. "Fine."

"So will you kindly tell your staff to treat me just how they used to treat me? And let me make the decisions for myself and my daughter."

He nodded. "Okay."

She turned and walked to the door, but before exiting she said, "And it would do you some good too."

"What?"

She cast a glance at him. "You know. Make your own lunch once in a while." She left before he could respond.

***

Rick stared at the space where Tara had been, wondering what he'd gotten himself into. He'd wanted to see what she'd be like when she came out of her shell. Now he knew. She was pigheaded, strong-willed, and basically infuriating.

And he was stuck with her.

He blew out a breath, walked back behind his desk, and sat in his chair. Oh well. He'd only have to be seen with her a few times, right? Pose for some pictures at the wedding. Be seen in Bora Bora for their honeymoon. The rest of the time he could avoid her.

He scrubbed a hand over his unshaven face. He needed a drink, but he'd promised Phil he'd stay away from the booze.

He pulled up his social media accounts on the computer and tapped the desk with his index finger. What should he post that would hint at things to come?

After a moment of thought, he typed:

Have you ever fallen for someone who works for you?

There. That would get people talking and start some speculation. The photos of him and Tara in her work uniform were already out there. It wouldn't take long for people to put two and two together.

His feed began lighting up with responses. Some were humorous:

Yes, but my wife didn't like it too much.

Some were more along the lines of what he was hoping for:

Who has your heart, Rick?

I'll work for you any day.

Is it serious, Rick?

He answered the last one.

It might be.

He smiled as more responses came in, some lamenting that he might not be single anymore.

Some offering to take her place. Some making fun of those groveling for attention.

His phone chimed and he pulled it out. It was a text from Phil.

You and Tara have dinner reservations tonight. Dress nice. I've made sure the paparazzi will be there.

He held in a groan. So much for avoiding Tara. Now he had to go tell her about the reservations, and by the way she acted earlier, he wasn't sure she would like it. He stood and turned off his monitor. Maybe she'd gotten over it by now. Either that, or she'd insist they stay home and make sandwiches.

He found her in the guest bedroom, playing with her daughter. A foam puzzle of some cartoon character lay spread out on the floor. Tara didn't see him come in. He watched her as she patiently let her daughter try different pieces until one fit. "Good job," she said, smiling.

He hadn't seen a genuine smile on her face before now, and it fascinated him. It changed her whole countenance. She looked sincerely happy, and he wondered what he could do to produce the same effect.

She turned and saw him and the smile faded. "What do you want?"

Nope. Still hadn't gotten over earlier. He shoved his hands in his pockets. "Phil has secured reservations for us. We are to go out and be seen. Sorry. I didn't know about it until now."

She drew in a breath, letting it out slowly. "It's what I signed up for, I guess. Who will watch Kylee tonight?"

"I've already hired a girl. You'll like her. Her name is Amanda. She'll be here soon."

The little girl frowned. "I want you, mommy."

"I know, darling, but I have to work tonight." Tara smiled at her daughter. "You'll have fun with Amanda. You can teach her how to put your puzzle together."

Kylee stared at the floor, and then big tears rolled down her cheeks. Rick was stunned. He'd never seen a kid silently cry. He'd seen plenty of temper tantrums, especially in public. The kind that grated on your nerves and made you want to toss the kid out the window. But this was different. She just stood there, fat tears streaming down her face, and it was breaking his heart. He knelt beside her. "Hey, it's okay. Why don't you show me how your puzzle works?"

She turned away from him and put her hands up to her face. He picked up two pieces that obviously didn't fit, and shoved them together. "Is this how it goes?"

She peeked through her hands, then laughed. "No!"

Her infectious laugh was the sweetest thing he'd ever heard. He smiled and chose two other mismatched pieces. "How about this?" He shoved them together.

Her giggle filled the room. "No!"

Out of the corner of his eye, he saw Tara hide a smile. It wasn't like the one she'd given her daughter, but he still felt a bit of satisfaction from being able to bring one out at all. He continued to match the wrong pieces until Kylee picked two of them up and showed him how they fit together.

"Do it like this." She patted him on the shoulder.

He grinned at her. "Oh, I see. Like this."

He put one sideways into another piece, and she giggled. "You're so silly."

"Why? This isn't how it goes?"

She laughed. "No!"

He scratched his head. "I swear that's how I learned it in puzzle school." He thought he heard a snort come from Tara's direction, but when he looked, her face was serious. It didn't matter. He was getting the little girl to laugh, and he was quite enjoying it.

Kylee plopped down on his lap and put her hands on his face. "You're funny."

Good. At least he'd won one of them over. "So is Amanda."

Her eyes lit up. "Is she as funny as you?"

"Oh, yes. And she wants to play with you tonight."

She stood and picked up several puzzle pieces. "Okay. I will play with Manda tonight."

That was easier than he'd thought. He got up from the floor and patted Kylee on the head. "You'll have fun." He turned to Tara. "Phil said to wear something nice. I guess I should go put on a suit."

She nodded, then mouthed, "Thank you."

He left, feeling like he'd won something, although he couldn't figure out what.

Chapter 4

ara slipped into her evening gown and twisted in front of the mirror. Getting dressed up to be seen in public was all a little too reminiscent of her days with Bobby, and it turned her stomach. Would the paparazzi recognize her? Still, she'd agreed to it. She had to.

She pulled her hair back in a French knot, pinning it in place, and allowed a few strands to fall. After she finished applying her makeup, she spritzed perfume and slipped into heels. Grabbing her clutch, she took one last glance in the mirror. Showtime.

She exited the master bathroom. Kylee and Amanda were sitting on the floor playing with Barbie dolls. When Amanda had arrived, Tara had spent some time talking with her. As a young college student, Amanda had taken the nanny job so she could help pay for school. She was bright and loved kids. Tara felt confident Kylee would get along great with her. She kissed her daughter on the top of her head and smiled at Amanda. "I don't think we'll be late."

"That's fine. You guys have fun." Amanda curled her hair behind her ear and grinned. "We'll play for a while, then have dinner, and I'll put her to bed."

"See you later, pumpkin."

"Bye mommy," Kylee said, not even bothering to look up.

Tara walked out into the hall just as Rick was coming out of his bedroom. She forced herself not to suck in a breath. He was movie star material in jeans, but he was even more handsome in a suit. If this were a Jane Austen movie, there'd be a lot of swooning going on. But she reminded herself that putting a suit on a pig didn't make it a man.

He looked her over and smiled. "Hey."

Suddenly self-conscious, she tightened her hold on her purse. "Are you ready?"

"Yes." He placed his hand on the small of her back, and tingles ran up her spine. She hurried ahead of him, out of reach. It was best to stay in a business arrangement with Rick Shade.

They got in the limo. The conversation was all surface as they rode, and soon they pulled up in front of a restaurant. Paparazzi waited along the sidewalk. Rick climbed out first and took her hand. Flashes of light blinded her as she stumbled out of the car.

Someone shoved a microphone in front of Rick's face. "Is it true you're dating your maid?"

Rick put his arm around her and pulled her close. "I met this lovely young woman in a rather unusual way, yes."

"Is this the girl that will tame your wild side?"

"Is it serious, Rick?"

"How long have you been dating?"

Rick put his hand up. "Not long enough. I'd like to continue dating, if that's okay with you." He gave them a drop-dead gorgeous smile, and then ushered her into the building.

They were led to a secluded part of the restaurant and were seated at a table near a large window, where the paparazzi could take photos of them while they ate. Tara felt like an animal at the zoo. This was worse than anything she'd endured while married to Bobby. His fame had been brief. Rick Shade was in a whole different category.

"Don't be nervous." Rick reached across the table and took her hands in his. "Just keep looking at me. It will make it easier to pretend they aren't there."

He smiled at her, and she realized he was a fantastic actor. Anyone outside on the sidewalk would see a couple being affectionate. She tried to smile back. "Okay."

The server brought them water and menus. Tara's stomach was tied in so many knots, she wasn't sure how she would choke down a meal, but when he came back she ordered anyway. It was expected of her. When they were alone again, she tried to focus on Rick, just like he'd said.

She looked into his eyes and butterflies joined the knots in her stomach. Man, he had some amazing eyes. They were cool blue, like a winter sky. They seemed to have no end to their depths. She dropped her gaze before the intensity grew too much for her.

"What are you thinking?" he asked.

Busted. She wasn't going to tell him she was thinking about how beautiful his eyes were. She picked up her water glass and wondered if it would look odd if she doused herself with it. "It's a bit warm in here."

"I'll have them adjust the temperature." He started to stand, and she put up her hand.

"No. Don't. I'm fine."

He sat back down and peered at her curiously. "You are an enigma."

She made a face. "What do you mean by that?"

"They would cool the room if we asked, but you insist on remaining uncomfortable."

She didn't want to admit that his intense gaze was the source of her discomfort. "I don't want to trouble anyone."

"It's no trouble. People like doing things for me."

He seemed sincere. Did he not realize people bent over backwards for him because he was famous? Did he think he was just naturally liked by everyone? "Well aren't you all that and a bag of chips?" She clamped her lips together. What was she doing?

"I'm a realist. And the reality is people want to make sure I'm happy."

"And why do you think they do that?" Tara couldn't believe the words coming out of her mouth. She needed to shut up now, before Rick changed his mind and tossed her out on the street.

He shot her a cheesy movie grin. "They like me."

She wanted to say, 'They like your money,' but had the presence of mind to keep that to herself. "You're right. You're irresistible." She couldn't quite keep the sarcasm from her voice, though, and Rick's grin slowly faded.

Deciding it was best to change the subject, Tara asked, "How did you get into acting?"

"My father's in theater. Stage acting. I grew up on stage."

"He must be very proud of you."

A look crossed his face but he didn't say anything; instead he fiddled with his silverware, unwrapping it and placing his napkin on his lap. Okay, maybe talking about his father wasn't the best idea. She tried a different approach. "Was it difficult to break into the industry?"

He shook his head. "Not really. I was in a stage play and someone saw me. Asked me to audition for a movie. Things just exploded from there."

"How old were you?"

"Twenty-one. Old enough to hire full-time and still young enough to pass for a teen on screen." He looked uncomfortable talking about his early acting career, and she wasn't sure why. He squirmed on his chair. "And what about you?"

What about her? What did he mean? "How did I get into housekeeping?" She raised an eyebrow at him.

He waved a hand in the air, looking around for the server. "Sure, fine, if that's what you want to talk about."

The man rushed over to their table. "What can I get for you, sir?"

"I'd like a Johnny Walker Black. Neat."

"Yes, sir."

The server left and returned with his drink faster than Tara had ever seen. Rick picked it up and downed half of it. He turned back to her. "So, what led you to your fine career?"

Why was he asking her about this? "After graduating from medical school, I decided I didn't want to be a brain surgeon. I realized cleaning toilets was my passion."

Rick threw his head back and laughed. "Okay, so that was a dumb question." His gaze rolled over her, a slight smile on his lips. "Did you go to school?"

"Bobby and I married right out of high school. He went to college and I worked so we could pay the bills." She swallowed back the sting that always came when she thought about missing out on college.

"And then the kid came along."

She bristled. Her daughter had a name. Why wouldn't he use it? "Yes. *Kylee* was born and I struggled to take care of her and pay the bills while Bobby finished with school. But then he graduated and landed an agent right away. I thought things would get better. He got the part in a big movie . . . and well, things went downhill from there."

"But the money helped, right?"

She held in a snort. "The money ruined my marriage."

Rick raised an eyebrow and picked up his glass, the amber liquid swirling. "I have a suspicion that Bobby had a little something to do with that." He took another drink.

"The instant fame changed him. I married a sweet man from the Midwest. I divorced a jerk who no longer cared about family values."

"He was what, nineteen when you got married? How's a nineteen-year-old kid supposed to know what he wants out of life?"

Tara didn't want to admit they were eighteen when they got married. "You're right. We were too young. I shouldn't have married him."

"And now you're stuck with the kid." He finished his drink and raised his hand to signal for another one.

Fury swept through her and she fought to control her face so no one got a photo of her in an outrage. "Listen. *Kylee* is the one bright light in all of this. I am not 'stuck with her.' She is my whole world, and if you don't stop calling her 'the kid' I'm going to cram that fork so far down your throat you won't see it until next year."

Rick's eyes grew wide. "I'm sorry, I didn't mean anything by it. You're just young, and now you're saddled with—"

"Don't even say it." Tara held up her hand to silence him, then sat back in her chair and tried not to scowl. The server brought them their meals, which was a good interruption because she didn't want to listen to Rick anymore.

He took a bite of whatever it was he ordered and smiled for the cameras outside. "Let's call a truce. I won't mention your daughter again and you won't sock me when we get back in the limo."

Sounded good to her. "Fine." She picked up her fork and pushed the food around her plate.

Her stomach now burned and there was no way she'd be able to eat anything.

After a few minutes, Rick pointed to her plate. "You don't like it?"

"I'm not hungry."

"Then we'll take it home. I'm sure you'll want to eat it later." He went to raise his hand but she stopped him.

"I'm fine. Let's just sit here and eat. It's what we came to do." She forced herself to smile.

He shrugged. "Okay." He ate his dinner in silence. When he swallowed the last of his drink he signaled the server. "I'll take another. Make it a double."

Tara frowned. "If you don't stop, I'm going to be carrying you home."

His laughter rang out, loud and boisterous. "You're funny." He ignored her warning and downed his third drink.

A slow panic started to build in her. What if he got drunk and embarrassed himself? Was she supposed to stop him?

He looked at her with interest. "What are you thinking?"

She wasn't sure what she was supposed to say to that. "I'm worried about you."

His face screwed up in puzzlement. "Me?"

"You're drinking too much."

He waved his hand. "You're too uptight. Relax a little." He sat back in his chair and draped his arm over the back.

"I think you're a little too relaxed."

"Life isn't meant to be taken so seriously."

She sighed. Nothing she said was going to change his mind. He was a grown man. He could do what he wanted.

A teenage girl timidly approached them, a pen and a paper napkin in hand. She couldn't have been older than thirteen. "Mr. Shade? I'm sorry to bother you. Could you sign my napkin?"

Rick turned to her, his movie star smile in place. "Of course. What's your name?"

"Jenny."

He scribbled something on the napkin and handed it back to her.

She read it, blushed, and said, "Thank you." She turned and ran back to her table.

"What did you write?"

"I wrote that she has a beautiful smile, and signed my name."

Tara heard the young girl squeal from across the room. "That was very kind of you."

Rick pushed his empty plate away and laid his napkin on the table. "My dad was hard on me as a kid. I was never good enough. But an actress once told me I had a nice smile. I can still remember her face and where I was standing when she said it. When I was feeling bad about myself, I'd think, 'at least I have a nice smile.' I figure, if I can give a memory like that to a kid, I've helped them in some small way."

Tears pricked at her eyes and she had to blink them away. Rick had a soft side to him. Maybe she'd judged him prematurely. He'd probably done just what he said, made a memory for the girl that would last her lifetime. She looked down at the table, unable to say anything.

Rick raised his hand and asked for the check. After he paid, they stood. Rick wrapped his arm around her as they walked, and her heart started doing a funny dance in her chest. Why did being close to him make her feel this way? Cameras flashed in their face outside. Rick ignored the reporters asking more questions about their relationship, and just gave them another stellar smile.

The limo pulled around the corner and Tara ducked as Rick waved at the cameras. Tara waited until he climbed in the vehicle, then she slid in beside him.

Rick leaned his head back on the seat and closed his eyes.

As the limousine pulled out into traffic, relief poured over her. They were no longer in the public eye. Rick hadn't done anything that would end up splashed all over the tabloids. She took a deep breath and let it out slowly, her shoulders starting to relax.

His eyes opened and he sat up. "Let's go dancing."

Tara shook her head. "I don't think that's a good idea."

Rick slid closer to her. "It'll be fun." He put his arm around her shoulders. "Carter, take us to a night club."

"I've got to get back to Kylee."

"Hey," Rick said, putting a finger on her lips. "We promised not to talk about her."

She ignored the tingling feeling coming from the contact and pulled his hand down. "No, *you* promised not to talk about her. I promised not to clobber you in the car, but I may have to break that promise if you get any closer."

He chuckled, but slid over. "As you wish." Then he put on his dazzling smile. "But we're still going dancing."

Tara sighed and gave in, even though dread was settling in her stomach.

Chapter 5

ick awoke with another monster headache, and his phone playing "The Imperial March." He moaned and rolled over, burying himself under the pillow. Phil. Why was he calling?

After listening to the imposing tune stop and then start up again a couple of times, Rick reached over to the nightstand and gave in. "Hello?"

"I told you no more booze."

Phil sounded mad. Oops. He tried to remember what had happened last night. He'd taken Tara out to eat. He'd had a few drinks, but no more than he could handle. They got in the car and . . . wait. He'd changed his mind about coming home. They'd gone to a club. He'd had a few more drinks, and he couldn't remember anything else.

He blinked. Crud. He was still wearing last night's clothes.

He was afraid to ask, but had to anyway. "What happened?"

"You don't remember?"

"Just tell me."

Phil groaned. "You got plastered, then you crawled up on the bar, got down on one knee, and asked Tara to marry you."

Rick's mind reeled. "I did?"

"Yes. And now, instead of the classy, upscale proposal I had planned, everyone is talking about you getting sloppy drunk and asking your maid to marry you."

Why didn't he remember any of that? What else had happened? He tried to sit up, but felt sick to his stomach. "It's not so bad, right? I mean, I was going to propose anyway."

"This isn't good. You don't need more bad publicity, and here you go making yourself look like an idiot again."

His head pounded. He needed to get off the phone. "I'll fix it."

"You'll fix it by laying off the alcohol. I mean it. No more."

Rick sighed. "Yeah. Fine. Okay."

"You'd better. Or you can kiss your career goodbye." The silence on the line told him Phil had hung up.

He tossed his phone onto the nightstand and cocooned under the covers. Phil was overreacting. It wasn't a big deal. He was supposed to propose to Tara. He just did it early.

After lying there for another twenty minutes without being able to fall back asleep, Rick finally rolled out of bed and stumbled into his bathroom. He stood in the shower for a good half hour before he felt a little better. As he toweled off he used the intercom to ask for a cup of coffee to be brought up to him. Then he slipped into his boxers and jeans, and lathered up his face to shave.

A knock sounded on his door as he was finishing up. He called out to the other room. "Come on in."

He looked in the mirror, sliding the razor over his chin to catch the last of the stubble. Then he rinsed the razor. Why wasn't Eliza bringing him his coffee? He glanced at the doorway and froze. Tara stood there, holding his coffee mug, an unreadable expression on her face.

If he had known *she* would be bringing him his coffee, he would have put his shirt on. Her gaze traveled over his chest before she steeled herself and pressed her lips together.

His stomach churned under her scrutiny. "Hey."

"That's what you have to say for yourself?" She walked into the room and set the mug down on the counter with a thunk.

He picked it up and took a drink, the hot liquid running down his throat. Unsure of what he was supposed to say, he shrugged at her.

"I see. You're going to pretend last night didn't happen."

Frustration welled in him. "If you want to talk about last night, you might want to fill me in, because after we got to the club, it's all blank."

She huffed. "Figures."

"Phil told me I proposed. I didn't mean to mess that up, but we were going to go down that road anyway, so I don't see what the big deal is." He took another sip of his coffee.

"I'm not upset about the proposal," she said, quietly.

Oh no. What else did he do? Guilt surged in his chest, tightening his stomach. He reached for his t-shirt and pulled it on, giving him time to think of what he wanted to say. "I shouldn't have had that much to drink."

She frowned. "Yes."

He ran a hand through his wet hair. Why was she staring like that? "If you're not going to tell me what I did, then why are you here?"

"I thought maybe you'd know. But it looks like you were so plastered that you blacked out. So I guess we are where we are."

What did that mean? He wanted to shake her and make her tell him, but he took a step back. "And where's that?"

"Engaged." She turned and walked out of the room.

***

Tara wasn't sure why she didn't simply tell Rick what had happened the night before. Instead, she'd acted like a moody teenager. What was wrong with her? Why couldn't she just tell him he'd kissed her?

And she didn't understand why she was so angry about it. She'd agreed to marry him for a publicity stunt. It was only natural the public would have to see them kiss.

So, why did that kiss upset her so much?

She tried to push aside the memory of last night as she walked into the kitchen and sat down beside Kylee, but it didn't work. At first the club was annoying. Loud music played, and Rick pulled her out on the dance floor. They were both overdressed, and she felt out of place until the music slowed and Rick pulled her close. His cologne did funny things to her, not to mention the way his arms around her made her heart stutter. She looked up at him, and those clear, blue eyes mesmerized her. They swayed to the music, and Tara felt a growing connection with him. When his lips came down on hers, all she could do was close her eyes and get lost in the intensity of the kiss.

All her life she'd heard about kisses that made women weak in the knees, or sent them over a cliff, but she'd never experienced one until last night. Fireworks went off and everything. She felt like she could fly. That is, until it ended and Rick stared down at her, his eyebrows pulled together in consternation. Then he'd turned around and left her on the dance floor to get plastered at the bar. Classy.

She thought she'd convinced him to leave right before he'd climbed up on the bar and announced to the whole club that he was going to marry her. Then he'd proposed. Suddenly everyone had their cell phones out, snapping photos and taking video.

Tara had been mortified, but she was also stuck. She'd signed a contract. The only thing she could do was say yes, in front of all those people. She had to look excited, even though it made her look like a money grabbing nitwit, taking advantage of a drunk loser.

Dragging him to the car after that wasn't easy, and by the time they'd made it home his speech was so slurred he wasn't making much sense. She'd helped him up the stairs, slipped off his shoes, and put him to bed. Then she went into her room. Since it was so late, you'd think she would have fallen right to sleep, but instead, the kiss played over and over in her head.

Kylee scooped the last of her cereal into her mouth and looked up at Tara. "Can I go play now, Mommy?"

"Sure."

"Are you going to come play with me?"

"Yes. I'll be up in a minute, then we'll spend the day together."

Kylee's face lit up. "Promise?"

"Yes." Tara smiled as her daughter slid down from the stool at the breakfast bar and ran off. She picked up the bowl and walked to the sink.

Eliza opened a cupboard and took out a canister. "So, what really happened last night?"

Tara sent Eliza a sad smile. "He got drunk."

"That's not unusual."

Tara rinsed the bowl and shut off the water. What had she gotten herself into? "Do you think he's got a problem with alcohol?"

Eliza shrugged and looked to the floor. "I shouldn't be talking about this." She turned back to preparing lunch.

"Come on. Who else is going to tell me?"

A frown crossed her face. "I don't think he's an alcoholic, if that's what you're asking. I think he drinks to forget," she said softly. "And anyone who does that has a problem."

Tara contemplated that for a moment. Rick Shade wasn't what he pretended to be . . . the shallow party boy. She wondered what lay beneath the surface. "I agree."

The swinging door opened and Rick came in. "There you are. I've been looking all over for you. Phil called back. He wants us to do some damage control. We have to go." He closed his eyes and pinched the bridge of his nose.

Tara stiffened. "Go where?"

"Ring shopping." He turned and left.

Of course they had to go ring shopping. And of course it would be some big production in front of flashing cameras. Ugh. Why did she agree to do this? She held back an eye roll and followed him out. "What about Kylee? I promised her we'd spend the day together."

"Amanda can watch her."

"Wait." Tara grabbed Rick's arm and forced him to turn around and face her. "Didn't you hear me? I promised Kylee. I can't go back on my promise."

He pulled his eyebrows together. "It's not a big deal. It will just be an hour."

What was wrong with him? "I am not about to go back on my word to my daughter. She is at a very fragile place right now." After what Bobby did, the little girl needed stability. She needed to know she could trust her own mother.

Rick closed his eyes and rubbed his temples. "Please stop yelling," he said, his voice low.

"I'm not yelling. You're hungover."

He opened his eyes and looked at her. "Then bring her with us. It won't be a big deal."

Dread tightened in her chest. "But I don't want her in front of the cameras."

A sympathetic expression filled his eyes. He reached out and took her hand in his. Warmth enveloped her. "I'm sorry. I know you want to shield your daughter. I'll do my best to take the brunt of the attention."

She bit her lip, knowing she'd signed the stupid contract and had to do what Phil wanted.

Rick ran his thumb over her knuckles. "It will be okay."

Her heart jumped. She pulled away from him, gazing at the floor.

"Hey," he said, putting his hand on her shoulder. "The kid . . . Kylee will be fine. I won't let them harass her. Okay?"

She looked up at him, knowing she was stuck. She had to. "Alright."

Chapter 6

ick wasn't sure why Tara insisted that the kid couldn't be left with the nanny, but he figured the public would find out about her soon anyway. Might as well let them see her. He just hoped she didn't throw some awful temper tantrum. He didn't need a screaming kid making his headache worse.

He waited by the limo for Tara to come out. When she emerged from the doors wearing a skirt that flowed around her ankles and accentuated her slim figure, he tried not to stare. She really was going to melt America's hearts. Her sandals showed off her pink toenails, and then he noticed her daughter wearing a skirt and pink toenails as well. Tara carried a booster seat and began buckling it in place.

The kid smiled up at him, her little pigtails sticking up from her head. "Mommy said we're going shopping, and if I'm good I get ice cream."

Brilliant. Tara was smart to think of that. He grinned at her. "Sounds yummy."

They climbed into the car and the little girl turned to him. "Will you sit by me?"

"Sure."

She buckled herself into her booster seat then grabbed his hand. "You have to be good, or you don't get ice cream."

Her face was so serious when she said it, he couldn't help but laugh. The kid sure was cute. "I'll remember."

The girl watched out the window as they pulled into traffic. "What are we going to buy?"

"A ring for your mommy. We're getting married."

Tara's face paled. "Why did you say that?" she whispered.

He leaned over to her. "Because it's true."

"We shouldn't pretend it's real in front of Kylee. She'll only be disappointed when . . . you know."

"Well we can't tell her the truth. What four-year-old can keep a secret?"

Tara pressed her lips together and turned away from him. He'd upset her again. Nice. He was on a roll. "Sorry, I just think—"

"No, you're right. I was hoping to spare her feelings, but I don't think we can."

How broken up could the kid be about them splitting? Rick nodded sympathetically, even though he didn't think the girl would care much one way or the other.

Kylee squeezed his hand. "Are we going to the mall?"

"No, we're going to a jewelry store." He turned to Tara. "Phil told the media, so there should be photographers."

"Okay." Her eyes didn't meet his, and he wondered if she was still upset about whatever his drunk-self did.

"Listen, about last night." She stiffened, but he continued. "I'm sorry. Whatever I did . . . I didn't mean it."

She swallowed, still staring out the window. "I know."

Man, he must have been a jerk. He nudged her and gave her what he hoped was an apologetic smile. "Forgive me?"

Her lips pressed together in a tight line. "Already forgotten."

They pulled up to Tiffany & Co. and Carter opened the door. Paparazzi camera flashes hit them as they got out of the car.

"Rick, is this your future bride?"

"Your fiancée has a child?"

"Do you regret your drunken proposal?"

"What are you going to do now?"

Kylee hugged her mother's leg and buried her face in the fabric of her skirt. Tara picked her up. Rick put his arm around Tara so they would look like a little family. "I don't regret anything. We're in love and getting married. We're here to pick out the ring."

He smiled at the camera to give them a good photo opportunity before leading her into the store.

An attendant in a suit immediately approached them. "Mr. Shade. Welcome. Right this way, sir." They were ushered into a private room where rings were brought out and showcased to them.

Tara held a perpetual frown and shook her head at each ring. Rick pulled the attendant aside. "Do you have anything bigger? These aren't very ornate."

"Of course, sir." They brought out another set of rings. She still shook her head at each one. Rick frowned. These rings were all five figures each.

What did she expect? He'd spend a few million on her rock? That wasn't part of the deal.

He leaned over to whisper to her. "What's wrong? Don't you like anything they have?"

"They're all too big. Gaudy looking. Don't they have anything simple?"

Rick stared at her. She wasn't fishing for a bigger ring. She wanted something smaller. He could barely believe it. "I'll ask."

He pulled the attendant aside again and apologized, explaining what Tara wanted. The man nodded, happy to oblige. He brought in another set of rings, this time much smaller. The man picked up one with his gloved hands. "This one is particularly lovely, set in a platinum gold band. The wedding band nestles into it. Its simple elegance is appreciated by all."

Tara smiled and touched Rick's arm. "I love it."

Rick took it from the attendant and slid it on her finger. Electricity zinged between them. He met her gaze, which seemed to hold an unspoken question. Had she felt it too?

The ring fit her finger perfectly. "This is the one," he said to the attendant.

He paid for the rings. Tara kept the engagement ring on her finger, and they gave him the wedding band in a velvet box. The whole thing was done in under thirty minutes, which was good because the child looked bored and walked around the room the whole time, patting the chairs and muttering under her breath.

Tara reached her hand out to Kylee. "Are you ready to go get ice cream?"

Her face lit up. "Yes!" She ran to her mother and grabbed her hand.

His phone rang and he glanced at the screen. Phil. He picked it up. "Hello?"

"I'm setting up an engagement photo shoot. What time works for you this afternoon?"

Rick just wanted to get all of it over with. "One o'clock."

"I'll make the arrangements. We'll shoot it in your home so it's more convenient."

"Fine, whatever." He hung up.

He was silent as they drove to get the ice cream. Kylee patted his arm. "The trees are tired today."

He looked out the window. "What?"

"They're tired. See? They aren't flapping to-day."

Rick wasn't sure what she meant. "Flapping?"

"The leaves were flapping yesterday, making wind. But they need to rest today. They worked hard yesterday."

She looked so serious, he wasn't sure how to answer her. Would it crush her to know the leaves flapping didn't make the wind? He decided to humor her. "Yes. I guess you're right."

Kylee continued to chatter as they drove. He wondered how she could have that much to say but not really say anything. They got out at the ice cream shop and several people took photos with their cell phones. He flashed a smile, then went inside. At least his headache had subsided. He sat in a booth and Kylee climbed up on his lap, snuggling into him. She smelled like strawberry shampoo.

Tara set a stack of napkins on the table and slid onto the bench opposite them. "Why don't you sit next to Rick? You're crowding him."

Rick had never had a little girl take to him before. In fact, he'd never been around kids much. He kind of liked her snuggling into him. "It's okay. She can sit on my lap."

Kylee looked up at him with adoration written across her face. "What ice cream do you like?"

"I like butter pecan."

Kylee wrinkled her nose. "Not chocolate?" Apparently the child couldn't comprehend anyone liking anything except chocolate.

He chuckled. "I like chocolate, too."

When they were done eating the ice cream, they traveled back to his home. Kylee fell asleep in her booster seat, and Tara had to lift her out and carry her up the stairs. She removed the little girl's sandals and put her in the guest bed. He still hadn't set up another room for the girl and felt bad that Tara had to sleep with her daughter.

When Tara was done covering up Kylee, she walked out and closed the door behind her.

"I can have the other guest bedroom set up tomorrow," Rick said.

Tara worried her lower lip. "I was going to talk to you about that," she said, her voice hushed. "Can she stay in my room?"

"Why?"

Her eyes darkened, and he wondered what was hidden behind them. "I just want to keep her close."

He walked with her down the stairs. "I don't understand."

Hesitancy slowed her steps. "I'm not being very . . . responsible. I don't want my own recklessness to hurt my daughter."

Rick stopped. "You think I would hurt her?" How could she think that of him?

"No, not like that." Her gaze dropped. "It's just that she's been through a lot. Her father . . ."

The thought of Bobby laying a finger on that little girl made his blood freeze. His hands involuntarily clenched into fists. "What did he do?"

"He turned into a different person after fame hit. He didn't physically hurt her. The stress of the part wore on him though. He was short with her. Made promises he didn't keep. Then, near the end, he just wasn't around anymore. He's supposed to spend a few weeks with her this summer, but so far he's made up excuses for why he can't take her. She keeps asking when she's going to see him. It breaks my heart. I want to be there for her. What I'm doing . . . this probably wasn't a good decision."

Moisture gathered in her eyes and she blinked it away. Rick didn't know what to do. Was he supposed to comfort her? Was it awkward to pull her into his arms when they barely knew each other? He ended up patting her on the back. "It's okay."

"No, I don't think it is. Her father abandoned her, and she's going to go through that again when we separate. I don't know what I was thinking." She rubbed her arms like she was cold.

"Listen. Kids are resilient. She'll bounce back."

That must not have been the right thing to say, because Tara stiffened and her mouth set into a hard line.

"And it's fine if you want her in your room. There's no harm in that."

She gave him a small smile. "Thanks."

They continued walking and he shoved his fists in his pockets. "Phil wants an official engagement photo to send to the papers. The photographer is coming at one."

"What should I wear?"

He wasn't sure what a person wore to an engagement photo shoot. "Something nice?"

"Okay."

Turns out he didn't have to guess what to have her wear. Phil came in before the shoot with a box full of designer clothes. All the top designers wanted Tara to be wearing their label for the photos.

When she came in the drawing room wearing a blue evening gown that hugged her curves, her hair pulled up, Rick's mouth went dry. She nervously clutched the necklace she wore.

The photo equipment was already set up. He stepped over an extension cord and around a light so he could take her hand, hoping to calm her anxiety. "You look lovely."

She glanced up at him. "You look nice, too."

The photographer ushered them to the other side of the room. "We'll start in here, then I'd like to get a few outdoor shots as well."

He photographed them in a few formal poses with Rick's arms around her, her hand on his arm so the public could see the engagement ring. The feeling of his skin against the soft silky dress was making his heart beat faster, and he wondered if Tara was at all affected by their close proximity.

"Now, kiss her," the camera man said.

Rick's breath caught. It was only logical that he would have to kiss Tara. They were getting married in the public eye. He just hadn't expected it yet. And he knew Tara well enough to know she wouldn't take such a thing lightly. He raised one eyebrow to silently ask her approval.

She gave him a subtle nod and then lifted her chin and closed her eyes. He brushed his lips against hers in a feather-light kiss. The softness of her lips combined with the feel of her in his arms created an intoxicating effect, and he inched closer. His heart raced and he was sure Tara could feel it under her fingertips, which were pressed to his chest. He kissed her again, this time more slowly, and his head begin to spin.

Kissing Tara was like nothing he'd ever experienced. It was longing and desire, wrapped up together in an intense heat. It brought back memories of kissing Scarlett, his ex, under the moonlight, only that had been a tiny flame compared to the raging fire now consuming him. The feelings invading him were unwanted and he pulled back, breaking the kiss.

A memory of last night came to him unbidden. He had danced with Tara, and he'd kissed her. He'd been playing it up for the camera, doing what he did best. Acting. But as they kissed, something changed. What started out as pretend soon turned real. He'd gotten wrapped up in it.

And that's why he'd gotten drunk and proposed.

He sucked in a breath. He'd done it to get the whole thing over with.

Tara looked up at him, a question mark on her face. He smoothed his features into a smile and turned to the camera man. "We done?"

"Not yet. Let's go get some outdoor shots."

They headed to the garden and took some more pictures. A few of them turned playful, and he knew they looked good for the camera. When the photographer said they were done, Rick nodded, let go of Tara, and turned to go inside. He didn't want to deal with anything at the moment. What he really wanted was a drink.

Chapter 7

ara followed Rick into the house and back to his office. Something was bothering him, and she wanted answers. She'd seen the instant change in him after the kiss. The same thing that had happened at the club before he'd gone off and gotten plastered.

He entered his office and opened a cabinet, pulling out a bottle. She should have guessed. She leaned against the doorjamb, one hand on her hip. "What do you think you're doing?"

He turned to her with a start, guilt showing on his face. He didn't say anything, so she continued. "You shouldn't be drinking."

"I promised Phil I wouldn't drink *in public*."

She raised an eyebrow. "Phil? What did he say about it?"

The guilty look intensified, and his hand wavered.

She crossed the room, not brave enough to take the bottle from him, but hoping she could talk him out of it. "Look, it's none of my business what you do after I leave. But while I'm here with Kylee, I think it's best if you put away the alcohol."

He stared at her, his expression clouded. Then he nodded and put the bottle back. He closed the cabinet.

They stood there for a couple of seconds, neither one speaking. Tara wasn't sure how far she should push him. Would he talk about it if she asked? She mulled over what she should say. Finally, she gathered up her courage to speak. "I've upset you."

"No, it's not you."

Tara allowed another few seconds to tick by. "Did you love her?"

A sad smile flitted onto his face. "Yes."

"Unrequited love is the worst."

His gaze hardened. "Yeah."

The way he said it meant that wasn't it at all, but she wasn't going to pry. He'd tell her if he wanted to. As he turned to leave, she stepped in front of him, an idea popping into her head.

"Kylee was asking if we could watch a movie tonight. Want to join us?" If she kept him busy, maybe he'd forget about whoever broke his heart.

He paused, and then nodded. "Sure."

"Okay. I'll feed her and we can watch it after that."

Rick stepped toward her hesitantly. "You could . . . eat dinner with me. I can tell Eliza to make enough for all of us."

He was reaching out to her, and she knew she should take hold of it, but she didn't want to back down from her principles. She wrung her hands, indecision running through her. "I don't want the staff waiting on me."

One side of his mouth pulled down into a frown. "You don't mind going to a restaurant, do you?"

"No."

"Why is this different?"

She was about to say that running a restaurant was their job, but she clamped her mouth shut. He paid the staff here, too. But for some reason it felt odd to have someone wait on her at home. She finally settled with a lame, "It just is."

He looked like he was trying not to smile. "Okay. Fine. I'll make dinner."

Her gaze snapped up to his. He was going to cook? Just to please her? The thought warmed her. "That would be nice. I can help."

"I'll give Eliza the night off."

That made her even happier. "I'm sure she would appreciate that."

Rick smiled and loosened his tie. "Then I'll go get changed into something more comfortable."

She nodded, delighted at the turn of events. "I'll meet you in the kitchen in a few minutes."

***

Tara changed into jeans and a comfortable shirt. She brought Kylee down to the kitchen. When she walked in, Rick was opening and closing cupboards, rifling through them. Kylee climbed up on a barstool, clutching her favorite Winnie the Pooh stuffed animal. Eliza stood against the far counter, her arms crossed over her chest, frowning.

"What are you looking for?" Tara asked.

Rick continued his rampage. "I found a recipe online for garlic chicken. Thought I'd make it. But I can't find the . . ." He looked down at his iPad. "Cornstarch. And Eliza's not being helpful."

"*You* want to make it, then *you* can find the ingredients." Eliza tapped her foot impatiently.

"We just thought it would be nice to give you the evening off," Tara said.

"I don't want the evening off. I've got a kid in college and tuition is due soon."

Rick glanced at her, a pained look on his face. "I'll make it a *paid* night off if you tell me where the cornstarch is."

She raised her eyebrows, then walked over to a cupboard he'd already rummaged through and grabbed a box. "Here." She shoved it at him, took off her apron and hung it on a hook. "Have fun."

After she left the room, Tara turned to Rick. "Why was she upset? What did you say to her?"

He made a face. "Why do you assume she's mad at me?"

"Well obviously she's not happy about something. And who gets mad about not having to serve you dinner?"

"Apparently Eliza," he said under his breath.

"Something else must be upsetting her. I'll talk to her later." Tara picked up his iPad and read the rest of the recipe. Together they pulled everything out while Kylee sat and spun back and forth on the barstool.

"You start searing the chicken and I'll measure out the ingredients." Rick handed the skillet to Tara.

She placed it on the stove and turned on the flame. After tearing the plastic wrap off the meat, she placed the chicken in the pan and went to find a spatula. The first three drawers didn't have what she needed.

"Did you see a whisk in those drawers?" Rick asked.

After rummaging to find his whisk and her spatula, a smoky smell stung her nose. "Oh, no. Something's burning."

She ran to the stove and picked up the skillet. Unfortunately, she picked it up too quickly and the chicken breasts went flying. One hit the tile floor and skidded under the stool where Kylee sat. The other bounced on the counter then fell to the floor.

Kylee clapped her hands and laughed. "Do it again, Mommy!"

Rick's lips twitched. "A new way of seasoning?"

"Yes. It gives your dinner a nice stone flavor." Her face heated as she leaned over and retrieved the meat. She turned on the faucet.

"Wait, what are you doing?"

"Rinsing the chicken. This isn't my first mishap in the kitchen, and I'm sure it won't be my last."

Rick frowned. "Why don't you throw them away? I'm sure there's more."

"That would be a waste. They're still good. Plus, your floors are cleaner than most people's tables." She stuck the chicken under the faucet and rinsed them off. "See? They're good as new."

His frown deepened. "And only a little burned."

"Exactly." She grinned at him. "No need to throw them away." She put them in the skillet and this time searched for the spatula before putting them back on the heat.

Rick shook his head, then turned around and continued to whisk his concoction. She thought she heard him mutter something that sounded a lot like, 'Crazy woman,' but she ignored him. Wasting good food was crazier than washing it off and using it.

After she was done searing the meat, she put it in an oven-safe dish and Rick poured the contents of his bowl over it. She put the lid on and slid it into the oven. She then sanitized the counter and the floor where the raw chicken had landed.

Rick stood there staring at her, but didn't say anything. She rinsed off the dishes they'd used, then turned to him. "Want to wash or dry?"

He looked at her with an incredulous expression on his face, one eyebrow raised.

"Come on." She whacked him on the arm. "It won't kill you."

"Fine. I'll dry." He opened a drawer and pulled out a dish towel.

Kylee grew excited as she saw the sink filling with bubbles. "I want to do dishes!"

"Okay, honey, you can help." Tara pulled Kylee's stool over to the sink so she could play in the bubbles. Tara grabbed a rag and washed the bowl Rick had used, rinsed it, then handed it to him. After he dried it and found where to put it away, she nudged him. "See? I knew you could do it. You're a domestic god."

He shot her a cheesy movie star grin. "I've been called all kinds of things, but I think that's a new one."

She stuck the skillet into the water. "Thank goodness there are no reporters here. *Rick Shade Puts Away a Dish* would be headline news."

He swiped his finger into the bubbles and smeared them on her nose. She laughed and scooped up a large pile.

"I didn't put that much on you. That's not fair."

"You started it." She came at him but he backed away.

Kylee giggled and shouted, "Get him, Mommy!"

She stood opposite him, waiting for the perfect moment to pounce. Kylee squealed and Rick turned his head. Tara took advantage of the distraction and jumped at him, smearing the side of his face with bubbles.

"Hey!" Rick grabbed her from behind, pinning her arms to her sides. She laughed as she tried to free herself.

"Oh, no," he said in her ear, his voice low. "You're not getting away with that."

Her heart thumped in her chest at his close proximity. "Okay, okay. I surrender."

He let her go and she ran to the sink, grabbing more bubbles.

The surprised look on his face, combined with the white mass of bubbles that had slid down his cheek and was now hanging from his jaw, made her giggle.

"You're not playing fair." He rushed at her and Kylee pealed with laughter. Tara took off around the other side of the island. Rick picked up a dirty measuring cup and scooped up some dish water.

"You wouldn't," she said.

"I would." He stood stone still for a moment. The second his arm began to move, Tara ducked. Greta entered the kitchen and got a face full of soapy water.

Greta gasped. "What is going on in here?" She wiped at the water on her face.

Kylee laughed and Rick picked up the towel and tossed it to Greta. "I'm sorry. That wasn't meant for you."

Tara couldn't help but join in Kylee's laughter. "Sorry, Greta," she said between giggles. She flicked the soap suds off her hand and into the sink. "We were just messing around."

Greta's gaze bounced between Rick and Tara for a moment before she said, "I see." She patted her face with the towel. "I just came to check on things. Eliza said you gave her the night off. Is everything okay?"

"Fine," Rick said.

"Her cooking has been to your liking?"

"Oh, good grief," Tara said. "Is that what she was worried about? We just wanted to make something ourselves tonight. Eliza is an amazing cook, but she doesn't have to wait on us hand and foot."

Greta nodded, looking at Tara. "Eliza said you wouldn't let her cook for you earlier, either. Will you be taking over the kitchen tomorrow as well?"

Rick looked over to Tara, like he was leaving the decision up to her. Tara didn't want to take over the kitchen. That was not what this was about. But apparently giving Eliza some time off was offensive. Seemed like no matter what she did, she lost. She sighed. "No."

"Very well." Greta tossed the towel on the counter and left the room.

"I feel like we've just been reprimanded," Tara said.

Rick laughed. "Maybe so." He came over to her and wiped her nose with his finger. "You still have some suds on you." His smile was genuine. Not the fake one he donned for the cameras. She liked how it looked on him.

"Thanks," she said, trying to breathe normally. "We'd better make the rice." She had to stop acting like a schoolgirl around him, or he'd think she had a goofy movie-star crush on him. Which was ridiculous. She had no such thing.

Chapter 8

ick stabbed a piece of chicken and put it in his mouth. Tara looked at him expectantly. "Any good?"

The salty flavor made him spit it back out into his napkin. "Ugh. It's terrible. I did something wrong."

"It can't be that bad." She put a bite in her mouth and immediately spit hers out as well. "Oh, way too much salt." She pushed Kylee's plate away from her.

"I'm hungry," Kylee said, reaching for the plate.

Nice. He ruined dinner and now the kid was going to starve. He stood. "I'll order pizza."

"Pizza!" Kylee clapped her hands.

Tara took the girl's plate and scraped off the chicken into the trash. Then she gave it back to her. "You can eat the rice and green beans."

Rick pulled his cell out of his pocket and dialed his favorite pizza place. It wasn't until he was in the middle of ordering that he realized he didn't know what the kid liked. He turned to Tara. "What does Kylee like on her pizza?"

"Plain cheese."

"Really? Plain?" He raised an eyebrow, but ordered it anyway after Tara nodded.

When he hung up the phone, Tara laughed. "You must not know many kids."

"Nope."

Tara tried to coax Kylee into eating her green beans, but the girl was shaking her head, lips pinched tight, pigtails swinging. "No, I want pizza."

"The pizza is coming. You can have some if you eat your green beans."

Kylee clamped a hand over her mouth and shook her head again. Rick held in a smile. There was no way Tara was going to get her to eat them.

Tara blew out a frustrated breath and wiped her forehead with the back of her hand. When she wasn't looking, Rick reached over and snatched a green bean and plopped it in his mouth. Kylee dropped her hand and her mouth formed a little 'o.' Rick winked at her and put his finger up to his lips while chewing up the bean.

Kylee giggled and Tara looked between them. "What did you do?"

He swallowed, put on an innocent face, and shrugged his shoulders. "I didn't do anything."

Tara looked away again and he plopped another bean in his mouth, exaggerating his chewing. Kylee laughed hysterically and Tara snapped her head around, her hands on her hips. "Now I know you're doing something."

He swallowed and shrugged again. "What?"

She looked down at the plate. "What are you doing with the beans? There were seven."

"Kylee must have eaten them."

Tara gave him a flat look, while Kylee shook her head and pointed at Rick. "He ate them!"

He opened his mouth in mock shock. "You told on me."

She giggled and Tara whacked him on the arm. "You're undermining my parenting."

He shot her an apologetic look. Then he got an idea. "Hey, Kylee. If you eat one, I'll eat one, and we can keep doing that until they are gone, and then your mom won't be mad at me anymore."

Her pig tails bobbed as she nodded and stabbed one with a fork. She popped it in her mouth and mimicked his exaggerated chewing. He chuckled. "Very good."

He ate another one, and waited for her to do the same. They took turns until they were gone, and Tara smiled. "Thanks."

He liked the way she looked when she smiled at him. He vowed to make her do it again. "You're welcome."

Tara washed the rest of the dishes; he dried and put them away. The pizza arrived, and they ate it in the kitchen. When they were done, Tara wiped the sauce off Kylee's mouth.

"You ready to see my theater?" he asked Kylee.

"You have a theater in your house?" Her eyes grew big.

"Yep. Come on, I'll show you." He reached his hand out and Kylee hopped down from the stool and took his pinky finger.

His theater was down a set of stairs, and he turned on the floor lighting when they got to the bottom. The room had an aisle down the middle, leather recliners in rows on either side. He led them to a cabinet in the back of the room. "What do you want to watch?" He opened it to show them his collection of DVDs.

Tara frowned at his case. "Not many kid-appropriate movies in here."

He pointed to one. "*Wizard of Oz*?"

"Too scary."

"*The Avengers*?"

She wrinkled her nose. "Too violent."

He lifted one shoulder. "We could stream something."

"Good idea. That's what I was going to do on my laptop." She pointed to the giant screen. "But this will be fun for Kylee."

They went to the front row where his leather couch sat. Rick picked up the remote and scrolled through the kids movies until Kylee pointed and grew excited. "That one!"

Tara sighed. "You want to watch *that* one? Again?" She was obviously displeased with the choice.

"Yes!" Kylee crawled up on Rick's lap. "Please?"

Rick leaned over and whispered in Tara's ear. "What's wrong with *Frozen*?"

"Nothing. The first twenty times." She gave him a tired smile. "But that's okay. Go ahead."

He clicked on the movie and it began. He had the strangest urge to put his arm on the back of the couch, like an awkward teenager watching a movie with his crush. What made that pop into his head? Was he thinking he'd put the moves on Tara? Sure, she was pretty. Beautiful, even. But she'd made it clear their relationship was not to be physical.

Kylee snuggled into his chest, her head tucked under his chin. He put his arms around her, mostly to keep them occupied and away from back-of-the-couch urges.

He enjoyed the movie more than he thought he would, and when it was done, Tara leaned over and whispered, "She's asleep."

He peered down and sure enough, Kylee had fallen asleep curled up on his lap. She looked like an angel, all sweet and innocent.

Tara stood, and he followed suit, cradling Kylee to his chest. Tara reached out for her daughter, but he shook his head. "I'll carry her," he whispered. She nodded and turned to walk up the aisle. Silently, he followed Tara up the stairs to the guest bedroom and laid Kylee on the bed.

"I'll get her in her pajamas," Tara whispered.

He nodded, and went into the hallway. He was about to head to his room when he found himself turning back to Tara. "Hey."

She looked up at him.

He didn't know how to tell her the evening meant something to him. Cooking the meal together, even though he'd messed it up, had been fun. He'd felt like they'd shared something. But how could he put it into words? He ended up just saying, "Thanks."

He wasn't sure she would know what he meant, but she smiled. "Sure thing."

He lowered his gaze. "Good night."

***

Tara shut the door and dimmed the light. Spending the evening with Rick had been nice. Different than she had thought it would be. He was more down-to-earth, somehow. She enjoyed messing around with him in the kitchen. In fact, it had felt a lot like flirting.

But that was silly, and she needed to put those thoughts out of her head and act more like a responsible adult. She slipped into her pajamas and crawled into bed. Maybe marrying Rick was impulsive and stupid, but she couldn't go back now.

She could, however, stop acting like a fool. He was a movie star and she was nobody. A year from now, he'd go on being a star and she'd go back to Iowa.

She closed her eyes but didn't fall asleep for over an hour. And even then, consciousness was right at the surface. Her brain didn't want to stop thinking about her evening with Rick.

Tara woke the next morning when someone small crawled on top of her. She opened her eyes to see Kylee two inches from her face. Morning light peeked in the curtains. Kylee put her hands on Tara's cheeks. "Mommy? Are you awake?"

"I am now."

Kylee didn't respond to her sarcasm. "Good. What are we going to do today?"

Her half-awake brain couldn't think of anything spectacular. "Take naps."

Kylee screwed up her face in disgust. "I don't want to take naps."

"I do."

"Can we go to the zoo?"

The thought of walking around the zoo in the summer heat didn't appeal to her. "I don't think so."

"The children's museum?"

Indoors. That had more promise. "Maybe."

"Yippee!" Kylee jumped down from the bed and ran into the bathroom. When Tara set out her clothes, Kylee frowned. "I want to wear my lady-bug shirt."

"That's fine. Go get it out of the drawer."

Kylee ran to the dresser and pulled the bottom drawer out and grabbed her favorite red shirt with black polka dots. It was getting small on her, but Kylee loved it, and Tara didn't have the heart to give it away just yet.

When they went down for breakfast, Kylee ran up to Rick who was sitting on a kitchen barstool. "We're going to the children's museum!"

Tara folded her arms. "I said maybe."

Rick smiled down at Kylee. "Ooh, that sounds like fun. Can I come?"

"Yes! You can play on the boat with me."

Tara sighed. "I guess we're going."

Rick turned puppy dog eyes on her. "Sorry, didn't mean to undermine you."

"That seems to be happening a lot lately." She couldn't get angry, though, and she smiled to show him she wasn't upset. With Rick going along to help her with Kylee, the children's museum sounded like it might actually be fun.

Her phone chimed and she pulled it out of her purse. A text from Bobby showed on the screen. She opened the text.

I want to see Kylee today. I have the day off. Call me.

She gritted her teeth. What was he doing? He couldn't text out of the blue and demand to see Kylee. He was supposed to take her last month so she could train for her new job. He hadn't had any time then. What made him think she would drop everything and rush Kylee over to him today?

Rick must have seen the look on her face, because he hopped off his barstool. "Everything okay?"

"No. I have to make a phone call."

Chapter 9

ick watched as Tara walked into the other room, her movements stiff. From the look on her face, she was about to chew someone out. He didn't want to eavesdrop, but . . . oh who was he kidding? He wanted to eavesdrop. Slipping into the hall behind her, he followed her until she went into the library. After a moment he heard her speak.

"Bobby. It's me. What do you think you're doing?"

She was talking to her ex. What did that creep want from her? He leaned closer to the doorway, his hand resting on the marble table in the hallway.

"You can't see Kylee today. We have plans." She blew out a breath of frustration. "I know you have a right to see your daughter. I just don't understand why you would suddenly text me that you have to see her today."

She listened for a minute, silent. "I know." More silence. "No, I don't want to go back to court."

He was threatening to pull her back into court? What a vile man.

"We're going to the children's museum." A pause. "Yes, I guess you could meet us there." Another pause. "Okay. We'll see you."

She sounded like she was getting done with the call, so he turned to go back. A pair of large brown eyes peered up at him. "What are you doing?" Kylee asked, her head cocked to the side.

He put his finger to his lips, then he picked her up. "I'm just making sure this is stable," he whispered as he tapped the table. "You can't be too careful with tables."

"Yes," Tara's voice said behind him. "It could tip over and hurt someone."

He turned around and put on a sheepish grin. "It might."

She gave him a flat look, but then turned to Kylee and forced a smile. "Your daddy is coming to play with you at the children's museum."

Kylee squealed. "Daddy's coming?" She clapped her hands together, and Tara's smile grew tight.

"Yes. So let's be on our best behavior."

Kylee put her hands on Rick's face and turned him so he was looking at her. "You'll play with me and daddy, right?"

Sure. Just what he wanted to do. Spend the afternoon with the jerk that dumped Tara. "Of course."

Kylee wriggled and when he set her down, she ran. "Let's go, Mommy! I want to see Daddy!"

"Okay, let's eat breakfast first."

Tara couldn't quite hide the frown on her face, and Rick wondered exactly what Bobby had put them through. Rick had his shortcomings, but at least he knew he wasn't a family man, and he didn't create one just to leave them on the side of the road. He clenched his jaw and shoved his fists into his pockets, then followed Tara back into the kitchen.

They ate cereal while Kylee told him about all the things at the children's museum. Some of the words he didn't understand, but he smiled and nodded anyway. She seemed most excited about getting dressed up and putting on a stage production for him. He admitted, by the time they were done eating, he was looking forward to it as well.

Since they weren't looking for publicity, he put on his favorite baseball cap and sunglasses that allowed him to blend into the crowd. Tara gave him a thoughtful look when he came out of his bedroom, but didn't say anything about his getup.

"You ready to go?"

He nodded. Kylee held her stuffed animal in one hand and grabbed his finger with the other, tugging him toward the stairs. "Come on, Rick. Walk faster."

Tara stopped them. "Kylee, we should leave Winnie the Pooh home. You don't want to leave him there."

Kylee clutched her stuffed animal to her chest. "But I want him with me."

Tara bent down. "Kylee, remember when we left him at McDonald's? We had to go back and you cried the whole time. You don't want to lose him again, do you?"

Kylee shook her head and handed Tara her toy. "No."

Tara put the bear in the other room and they were on their way. By the time they arrived at the museum, Kylee could hardly contain herself. "Where's Daddy?" she asked when they walked in the door.

Tara glanced around. "I don't think he's here yet."

A frown appeared on Kylee's face. "But he'll miss my play."

"I'm sure he'll be here soon." Tara swallowed, and Rick didn't miss the worried look she tried to hide. While they stood in line to pay, Tara glanced around every few minutes.

After they were admitted, Kylee tugged them toward the stage. "Is Daddy here yet?"

Tara shook her head. "Why don't you go get dressed up and check back in a few minutes?"

"Okay." Kylee ran behind the red curtain.

A boy in a diving mask pranced about the stage pretending to be underwater. A tired-looking mother clapped her hands in between trying to wrangle a toddler from escaping her grasp.

Rick and Tara sat on an empty bench and waited for Kylee. The boy in the diving mask ran backstage.

Rick nudged Tara. "Do you think Bobby will show up?"

"He was adamant about seeing Kylee today. I can't imagine he'd change his mind, but you never know with him."

"Why does he want to see Kylee?"

Tara twisted her fingers together. "I don't know."

Before he could think it through, he put his arm around her. "Don't worry. I won't let him hurt her."

"All he has to do is cancel and it will crush her."

As if on cue, her phone chimed, signaling a text message. She threw him a look, and then dug her phone out of her purse. Relief showed on her face. "He's here."

She fiddled with her phone, probably telling him where they were, because a moment later Bobby came strolling up to them. He stuck out his hand to Rick. "I'm Bobby Goodwin."

Rick stood and took his hand, simply because there was nothing else he could do that wasn't completely rude. "Rick," he said, introducing himself.

Bobby ignored Tara and sat down on the bench next to Rick. "Yes. I know who you are. I hear you and Tara are getting hitched."

The look on Bobby's face sent alarm bells through his head. What was this guy up to? Was he trying to get out of child support? "Yes."

At that moment Kylee came rushing out on stage wearing a tall princess cone on her head and a pink gown that was two sizes too big for her. When she saw Bobby, she squealed, "Daddy!"

Kylee ran to Bobby and embraced him. "You get to see my play!"

Bobby nodded. "Of course. Go up on stage." He shooed her away.

Kylee's smile looked like it would stretch off her face. "Okay!" She climbed back up on the short stage. The boy came out from behind the curtain wearing a green frog costume. A hood covered most of his head, sporting frog eyes and a wide mouth. He crouched down and began hopping around the stage.

"No, you have to stay by me," Kylee shouted to the boy.

Bobby turned to Rick. "So, what are you working on right now?"

Kylee hiked up her long dress and marched over to the boy, who hopped out of the way. "Stop! I have to kiss you and make you turn into a prince." The boy kept hopping and Kylee chased after him.

Tara laughed and clapped her hands. Rick smiled. "Bravo!" he shouted. A few passersby stopped to watch.

Bobby ignored the stage. "You involved in a film?" he asked, trying again.

Irritation swept through Rick. Wasn't the guy here to see Kylee? "No."

The frog gave up hopping and ran away from the princess, who was desperately trying to kiss him. A small crowd had formed around the stage and everyone laughed.

"Wait!" Kylee yelled. "You have to let me kiss you!"

The frog gave a panicked expression to the crowd and zig-zagged out of her way. Laughter filled the room.

"I'm between gigs too," Bobby said. "This industry is tough, isn't it?" He huffed and crossed his arms over his chest.

Rick ignored Bobby and clapped for Kylee. "You go, Kylee. You get him!"

The frog zigged when he should have zagged and Kylee flew into him. She wrapped her arms around him and planted one on the furry frog eye on top of his head. The crowd cheered.

The poor frog dropped to the stage and flopped around for a minute while Kylee backed up. Then he sprang up and wriggled out of his frog costume. "I'm a prince!" he yelled.

Everyone clapped except for Bobby, who looked annoyed that Rick wasn't paying attention to him. Kylee beamed and ran behind the curtain to put away her costume.

"Yep, this business is tough. I'm actually looking for a new agent," Bobby said. "You know how agents can be."

Rick didn't say anything. He just stared at Bobby.

"Any chance you could put in a good word for me? Maybe talk to your agent?"

So that's what Bobby wanted. He couldn't care less about Kylee. He found out Tara was marrying a famous actor, and he wanted to take advantage. Real nice. Rick glared at Bobby but didn't answer. No way was he going to help this idiot.

Kylee burst out from behind the curtain and ran to her father. "Daddy, did you see my play?"

"Yes. Now go put on a costume and do another one." He gave Kylee a little shove and turned back to Rick.

Tara frowned and her lips pinched, like she wanted to say something but was keeping her tongue in check. Kylee tugged on her father's hand. "But I want to go play on the boat now."

Bobby put his finger to his lips. "Hush, now. The grownups are talking."

A frown pulled Kylee's lips down, and she blinked back tears.

Rick stood, controlling himself so he didn't punch Bobby in the face. "I think we're done talking." He crouched down to Kylee's level. "Show me where the boat is. I want to see it."

Kylee recovered from her father's brush off and took his hand. "Come on. It's over here."

Tara sent him an appreciative glance. Bobby's face soured, but he followed them through the crowd toward the next exhibit. Kylee climbed into the boat filled with brightly colored balls. "You can jump in here," she said, demonstrating how to jump into the balls.

Rick ignored Bobby and took a step closer to Tara. "Great jump, Kylee."

Bobby stood silent for a few minutes while they watched Kylee play in the boat. When Kylee began chatting with another child, Bobby hitched up his pants and turned to Rick. "I know how this business works. It's not how talented you are, it's who you know."

Rick made a calculated effort not to walk away from the guy. "Is that so?"

"Yep." Bobby leaned onto the wooden rail. "And I also know you and Tara here want a nice wedding with nothing getting in the way."

Tara's cheeks flamed red. "Bobby, just stop it."

Bobby put his hands up in a surrender motion. "Hey, I want that, too. Wouldn't want to see anything hold you two love birds up."

Rick clenched his hand into a fist but held it by his side. "Are you threatening us?"

Bobby's eyes widened. "Threatening? I think you misunderstood me." He smiled, and an intimidating gleam came into his eyes. "I just want what's best for the two of you." He looked over at his daughter. "And Kylee."

The way he said Kylee's name, with menace, made Rick's stomach flip. Tara's eyes grew fierce. "You stay away from Kylee," she hissed, her voice low.

Bobby's smile took on an evil glint. "Now, how can I do that when she's my daughter? I have a right to see my own daughter."

Tara's hands shook and Rick pulled her close to his side.

"But, like I said, I only want what's best for her." Bobby shoved his hands in his pockets. "And I hope you want what's best for her, too."

He shot a meaningful glance at Rick before turning and walking away.

Tara's face drained of color and she looked up at Rick. "What's he going to do?"

Rick had no idea, but he wasn't about to let anyone mess with Kylee. "Nothing. He's not going to do a thing, because I'm getting a restraining order."

Chapter 10

ara held Kylee close and eased herself down on the pillows. She came upstairs to put her daughter to bed, but couldn't let her go just yet. Bobby had really shaken her up and caused Kylee a lot of distress.

Why had he left like that? She could have punched him in the throat. Didn't he realize what he was doing to his daughter? When Kylee noticed her father was gone, she started wailing. Huge tears rolled down her cheeks, and Tara had thought they would have to leave the museum because nothing would settle her down.

It was Rick who got Kylee to stop crying. He simply picked her up and patted her back. The gentle touch worked a miracle. Kylee's cry turned into a hiccup, and then she snuggled into his chest and closed her eyes.

After that, he distracted her by asking her to show him the rest of the museum. He was such a sport. He let Kylee drag him all over the place, and acted interested in everything she showed him. When they went into the miniature grocery store, he helped her fill her cart and check out. He made her laugh when he tried to climb into the small airplane, obviously made for kids. She was delighted when he danced to her "music" that she played on the instruments. Tara had to admit she giggled along with Kylee at his crazy antics.

When they were done at the museum, he'd taken them out to eat, and then they'd gone to the park. He'd pushed Kylee on the swings and ran around the playground with her. She loved watching them together. Kylee looked at Rick with such adoring eyes. Having a male role model around for her daughter was wonderful.

How was she ever going to thank him for what he did for Kylee? She kissed the top of her daughter's head and slid her under the covers. Kylee stretched and curled up to the pillow.

Tara put her hand on Kylee's back, not quite ready to leave her. Whatever Bobby had in mind, she couldn't let him use Kylee as a weapon. She worshiped her father. He could leave a permanent scar on her soul.

Rick stuck his head in the door. "You okay?" he asked, his voice quiet.

She nodded, even though that wasn't true. She wasn't okay. She was worried about Kylee and what her wretched ex-husband was going to do if he didn't get his way.

"Want to watch a movie or something?"

She smiled and nodded again. That was a good idea. It might take her mind off Bobby for a while. She rubbed Kylee's back one last time and then clicked off the light and followed Rick out into the hall.

"Want to see what's playing at the theater? Or stream something?"

She appreciated him giving her the choice. "I'd rather stay here, if you don't mind."

"That's fine. I'll have Eliza . . . I mean . . . I'll make some popcorn."

Tara laughed. "Sounds good. I'll find us some sodas."

Once they were settled on the couch in his theater room, snacks in hand, Tara let the tension release from her shoulders. Rick scrolled through the movie choices.

"We should watch one of yours," Tara said. She'd been half-joking, but after the words came out, she realized she hadn't seen one of his more recent movies, and it might be fun.

His eyebrows rose, and she couldn't tell if he was flattered or if the suggestion made him feel awkward. "Really?"

"Yes. I haven't seen *Living Dangerously*. Looked like a funny one."

He smiled, and it wasn't his fake one. This one made his eyes crinkle, like he held a secret and couldn't wait to share it with her. "Okay."

He started the film and she leaned closer to him to grab a handful of popcorn. Maybe that wasn't the smartest decision, because she caught a whiff of his musky cologne and nearly melted in a puddle. She stuffed the popcorn into her mouth so she could distract herself.

The film was one of those silly yet suspenseful stories about a regular Joe who got caught up in a conspiracy by accident. There were quite a few laugh-out-loud moments, and Tara found herself sucked into the story. In the middle of the movie his arm slipped down from on the back of the couch to over her shoulders. She should have protested, but it felt nice being close to Rick, so she left it alone.

It was a little surreal watching Rick on the big screen. He was a good actor. It was easy to get lost in the plot of the movie and forget she was watching the man sitting next to her.

After the movie, he clicked off the screen. "What did you think?"

She looked up at him. He had a vulnerability in his eyes, one she hadn't ever seen before. Was he nervous about her reaction to his film? "I liked it."

Another genuine smile formed on his face. "Yeah?"

"You're good at what you do."

He sobered. "People tell me that all the time."

"It's true."

He fiddled with a strand of her hair. "Usually they say it when they want something from me." His gaze met hers. "But with you, I know you mean it."

Tara blinked. She'd never thought about what it must be like to have everyone saying whatever they think you want to hear, just to get something from you. How would you know who to trust? She stared into his crystal blue eyes. How many times had he been hurt by people taking advantage of him? She let her gaze fall. "I do."

He leaned over and kissed the top of her head, then hopped off the couch. The gesture was sweet, but his immediate withdrawal from her made her think he hadn't meant to do it. "It's late," he said, not meeting her gaze. "I should let you get some sleep."

Her shoulders grew cold without his arm there. "Yes. I'm tired." She got up and picked up the empty soda bottles.

Rick grabbed the popcorn bowl and followed her up the stairs. "I'll call my lawyer tomorrow and get the paperwork started for the restraining order."

"Okay." It made her feel better knowing Rick was protecting her and Kylee. She fell asleep quickly, no longer worried about Bobby.

***

Rick paced his office as he clutched his phone to his ear. "What do I need to do to file a restraining order?"

His attorney's low voice came over the line. "Tell me exactly what happened. How did he threaten you?"

"He threatened to hold up the wedding, and he implied he might do something to Kylee." When Mike didn't answer, he added, "Tara's daughter."

"What were his exact words? And did anyone else hear this?"

"Tara heard everything. And he said, 'I wouldn't want anything to hold you up.' And, 'I just want what's best for the two of you, and Kylee.'" Saying it out loud to Mike made him feel foolish. It didn't sound threatening at all, so he added, "And the way he said it implied he'd do something."

Mike blew out a breath. "Is that it? Did he come at you or anything?"

Oh, this wasn't good. "No," he said, wishing the threats had been more . . . threatening.

"I'm sorry Rick; no judge is going to issue a protection order based on that. Maybe if the guy socks you one, or says he's coming after you with a gun, you can try for one. But what you have isn't really a threat. And the court is going to want proof."

Disappointment filled Rick. "What else can I do?"

"Keep records. Write down everything he said to you, and if you hear from him again, keep track of everything that happens. If he does something the judge can see as threatening, you'll want proof. If he hurts anyone, call the police and press charges. Things like that will help you get a protection order."

He had to let the guy harm Kylee before anything could be done about it? That was messed up. "Can I stop him from seeing Kylee?"

"You can send me the court-ordered parental plan, but from what you've said it sounds like you can't stop him from seeing his own daughter. Not unless he harms her and there's enough evidence to prove he did it."

"Alright. Thanks, Mike."

"Call me if anything else happens."

Rick agreed and hung up. Pent-up energy surged in him and he left his office and stalked down the hall. Maybe he was making this into a bigger deal than it was. Maybe Bobby was a jerk, but not capable of doing anything horrible. Tara had said he'd never hit Kylee or anything like that.

The thought that Bobby was all talk and no action gave him little comfort as he entered his workout room and hopped up on the treadmill. Setting the speed high, he started running. Bobby's face came into his mind. If there wasn't anything legal he could do to keep Bobby away, maybe he should just give in and have his agent call him. Throw him a bone. If that was all he wanted, maybe Rick would be better off to comply.

The idea made him angry, but he wanted Bobby to leave them alone. After he hit five miles, he slowed the treadmill down to a walk. The workout felt good, and he grabbed a towel to mop the sweat off his face. After his shower he'd call his agent and give Bobby what he wanted. Then he would tell Tara he'd taken care of things and maybe he could get another smile out of her.

Armed with a new plan, he hopped into the shower and allowed his tension to go down the drain. Once he was dressed, he called his agent and left a message, telling him to call Bobby. He felt a little slimy after hanging up, but he brushed it off. He then set out to find Tara. He didn't have to search long. The sound of a child playing the piano led him down the hall to the drawing room.

Kylee was sitting on the bench, gleefully pounding on the keys. Tara shot him an apologetic look. "Sorry, I hope it's okay if Kylee plays on your piano."

He smiled and slid onto the bench next to Kylee. "I don't mind."

The little girl stopped playing and threw her arms around his neck. "You're here!"

"She's been asking for you all morning," Tara said.

"She has?" Why would Kylee want him?

Tara nodded and Kylee sat back down beside him. "Listen to my song, Rick." She began pounding on the keys again. After a few moments, she stopped and looked up at him.

"Very nice, Ladybug," he said, ruffling her hair and still wondering why the girl would be asking for him.

Kylee started back up, and he sent a questioning glance at Tara, who just shrugged. When Kylee tired of playing the piano, she slid off the bench and grabbed Rick's hand. "Come play with me."

Tara protested. "I'm sure Rick has lots to do—"

"It's okay. I don't mind." The last thing he wanted to do was brush off Kylee like Bobby had done. He allowed the girl to pull him out of the room and up the stairs.

Tara's bedroom floor was littered with plastic pieces to some kind of pipe system. Kylee pulled him to the carpet. "Let's play marbles!"

He wasn't sure what she meant, but when he looked at the pipes and ramps he realized they created a system for the marbles to fall through and run along. He helped her fit some pieces together, and soon they were building a grand structure.

Tara sat on the bed watching them. "How did it go with your attorney?"

"There's a slight snag. We can't get a restraining order. But I think I've taken care of things." She lifted one eyebrow but didn't ask him about it further, which was good. He didn't want to tell her he'd pretty much given in to Bobby.

Chapter 11

ara could tell Rick was hiding something by the way he sidestepped her question. But she didn't want to pry. There wasn't much they could do, anyway. If Bobby wanted to make trouble, he would. A restraining order wouldn't stop Bobby from messing with their lives—especially since he was due three weeks with Kylee, and he could take her back to court if she didn't give it to him. She didn't need any more court costs piling up.

She watched Rick build the marble maze structure with Kylee, her heart going out to him. He made Kylee giggle, endured her hugs, and let her climb all over him. It was endearing how he patiently helped her put the pieces together. He probably had no idea what he was doing for her.

She needed male bonding, especially after her father withheld that from her for so long.

But what would happen when she and Rick went their separate ways? The thought made her stomach sour. Maybe it wasn't smart to let her daughter bond with Rick. Was she just setting her up for more heartbreak later? Tara pushed the thought out of her head. She couldn't dwell on that. Kylee needed Rick right now.

Rick's phone played the *Star Wars* Darth Vader tune. She gave him a quizzical look, and he just shrugged and answered it. "What's up, Phil?"

His mouth pulled down into a frown. "Which website?" Rick stood and paced the room.

Tara's throat tightened. What was wrong? She watched the tense expression on Rick's face.

"Alright, alright. We'll take care of it. Issue a statement or something." He paused. "Why wouldn't that work?"

A sinking feeling started in Tara's stomach. Whatever happened wasn't good. Rick spoke to Phil for another minute before hanging up and letting out a frustrated grunt. "We've got to go make another appearance tonight."

"Why? What happened?"

"Someone snapped a photo of us yesterday at the museum. I'm glaring at you, and Bobby is behind me grinning. It looks like we're having a fight. A website ran a story about how we're breaking up and you're going back to Bobby."

Tara snorted. "That's ridiculous."

"Well, I know that, and you know that, but people believe what they read online. Even if it's a stupid celebrity site. Two other sites already repeated the story."

"What did Phil say about issuing a statement?"

Rick frowned and scrubbed his hand over his stubble. "Statements don't mean anything. The damage is done. The only way to combat the rumors is to go out and be seen together." He gave her an apologetic look. "Guess we're going out tonight."

Tara sat down next to Kylee. "Alright." If she had to leave Kylee with Amanda again, she'd spend as much time as she could with her during the day. Kylee climbed up on her lap and chattered about the marbles.

Rick hesitated, a look on his face telling her there was something else.

"What?" she asked him.

"Phil thinks we should go to the screening for the new Bradly Cooper film, then be seen together at the celebrity bash afterward."

She still didn't understand the look on his face. "Okay."

"It's in Las Vegas."

Nice. Just what she wanted to do. Run off to Vegas and leave Kylee with the sitter for who knows how long. "When do we need to leave, and when will we be back?"

"We'll take my jet. We'll probably need to get ready to go now. The party will last well after midnight. We'll get a hotel so we can get some sleep and fly back tomorrow."

Tara stroked Kylee's hair. She'd never been away from Kylee overnight before. Would she have trouble falling asleep? Would she cry? Tara steeled herself and slowly nodded. "Alright. I'll get ready."

***

Tara's heels clicked on the concrete as she walked with Rick toward his plane. Heat rose off the pavement and stung her eyes, blurring her vision. Or maybe it wasn't the heat. Maybe it was the fact that she was leaving Kylee with a babysitter she barely knew for an overnight excursion. Whatever the cause, she blinked the moisture back.

Rick glanced at her. "You okay?"

"Fine." She ran a hand down her little black dress. It was one she'd bought back before Bobby had made it big. They hadn't had a lot of money, but she'd splurged so she could look nice for the shindigs Bobby wanted to take her to.

The closet in Rick's guest room had magically been filled with designer outfits. Some of them came from the photo shoot. Others Rick had his assistant pick up. She swallowed her annoyance and just wore what she was comfortable in. Rick was only trying to be helpful. He couldn't understand that she didn't want anything to do with the lifestyle Bobby left her for.

Rick slid his hand down her back, sending involuntary shivers through her. "Kylee will be fine."

How did he know what she was thinking? She nodded and took a calming breath. "I'm sure you're right."

He stopped at the steps and held out his hand. She grasped it and he helped her up the stairs. The plane looked small on the outside, but she was amazed at how much room there was when she boarded. Two leather couches faced each other along the sides, a coffee table in the middle. A bar with three mounted barstools took up the back wall, and a small hallway lead further back, where she supposed the bathroom was situated. Rick motioned to a couch. "Have a seat."

She slid onto the chair and almost moaned at the way the soft leather conformed to her body. Rick sat next to her, his arm on the back of the seat behind her. "You look tense. Want a drink?"

"No." She gave him a flat look, which he ignored.

"The screening starts at six. There will be a red carpet outside the theater. Don't worry about it, just stop and smile for the cameras before heading in the door."

Cameras. Lights. Glamour. Shallow people. All things she despised. She focused on a mental image of Kylee and pushed the rest out of her head. Kylee was the reason she was doing all of this. Nothing else mattered. "Sounds good."

Rick eyed her. "Is being with me really that terrible?"

His voice was soft. Almost raw. She looked into his eyes and her world tilted. She needed to remember not to do that. She couldn't fall for

Rick. "Of course not. I'm just worried about Kylee. That's all."

He squinted at her. "It's more than that."

How did he do that? She brushed a strand of hair back from her face, trying to decide if she wanted to spill her guts to him. "You wouldn't understand."

"Try me."

She picked at her fingernail. "Nothing against you or whatever, but I can't stand the Hollywood glitz. The putting on a show for others. The shallowness of it all. I really hate it."

He nodded. "I get it."

"Do you? Because you sure seem to love it all."

Rick looked down at the carpet. The engines on the plane came to life, and surprisingly they were quieter than she expected. Rick's fingers grazed her shoulder and he looked into her eyes. "I don't think it's the glamour as much as it's the memories it brings you."

"What does that mean?"

"Your husband left you for the Hollywood life." He spoke so quietly she almost couldn't hear him. "That had to hurt you deeply. You loved him." He stared at her, his gaze penetrating. "With all your heart."

His words pierced through her, causing her throat to constrict. She blinked back tears. He was right. She'd been so mad at Bobby for what he'd done, she hadn't stopped to really process it. "I gave him everything I had. My heart. My soul."

"And he ripped them away."

The plane began taxiing down the runway. Tara gripped the leather seat, her throat dry. "I supported Bobby through all the hard times. I scrubbed toilets so he could go to school. I took care of Kylee, did all the housework, and budgeted every penny so he could live his dream. And what thanks did I get? He ran around behind my back. The media knew about his affair before I did. I only found out because my friend . . ." Her voice broke, the memory of that phone conversation crushing her once again.

Rick slipped his arm around her shoulders and pulled her to his chest. "He didn't deserve your love."

A choking sob escaped before Tara could rein in her feelings. Rick reached behind her and procured a tissue from somewhere hidden to her view. She grabbed it and dabbed at her eyes. She didn't want to smear makeup all over his white shirt and tie.

Rick rubbed her back, his warm hands making her feel things she didn't want to feel. Why did she have to have a crush on her employer? Their stupid plan would be so much easier if she could distance herself from him. But no. She had to erupt in tingles every time he touched her. And he had to go and turn into a nice guy who listened to her.

She leaned her head on his shoulder and let him comfort her, even though it wasn't a good idea. But it felt too good not to allow the one small luxury.

"Not everyone is like your ex," he whispered in her ear.

Pain stabbed through her at his words. What was he implying? That he wouldn't cheat on her with their fake marriage? That he wouldn't have left her had he been in Bobby's place? Or was he simply trying to console her?

She pulled away from him and blew her nose. "Thanks," she said, no other words coming to her.

He gazed at her, and the depth of emotion in his blue eyes made her catch her breath. He looked like he was going to say something else, but leaned back and broke eye contact instead.

The intercom system clicked on and the pilot told them they'd be taking off soon. Rick motioned for her to buckle her seatbelt. She hadn't even noticed the couch was equipped with them.

She drew in a deep breath and let it out slowly. Well. Now what should she say after that sorry display? Maybe keeping her mouth shut from now on would be a good idea.

Rick ran a hand through his hair. "Do you want a bottle of water?" He motioned to the cabinet behind them. "There's soda, too, if you prefer."

Glad for the change in subject, she nodded. "I'll have a water."

He opened the cabinet and scanned the contents. "Huh," he said, as he pulled out a water bottle for her.

"What?"

"Phil must have called the staff. The booze is gone."

Tara shrugged, hoping she appeared like she didn't care either way, when really, she was relieved. They certainly didn't need another drunken display like Friday night.

Chapter 12

Rick unabashedly stared at Tara as the plane took off, studying her face and the way a few tendrils of hair curled down by her ears. He wanted to pull the silver clip out of the back and let her hair spill down around her shoulders. Actually, what he really wanted to do was kiss her again, but that was a bad idea. He didn't want to get all tangled up in a relationship with her. She wasn't like the other girls. Tara's heart ran deeper.

Tara shot him a questioning glance, and he turned his gaze away. It was for the best, anyway. He shouldn't be thinking about her. He should be focusing on his career and how to get it back on track. He'd make small talk to pass the time. "Have you ever been to a special preview screening before?"

"Yes." She twisted her hands in her lap. "Bobby's film."

Of course. Why did he ask her that? Stupid. Should he ignore her stricken look or apologize? He decided to move on. "Would you like to Facetime with Kylee when we land?"

Her eyebrows shot up. "I'd love that."

"We should have enough time before we need to be at the theater."

She smiled at him, and he marveled at the way it made her eyes light up. They chatted about nothing important for the rest of the flight, Rick keeping to subjects he figured wouldn't have Bobby memories attached to them.

After they landed he pulled out his cell and called Amanda. When they had Kylee on Facetime, Rick put his arm around Tara so Kylee could see them both.

"Rick!" Kylee squealed. "Manda and I made cookies!"

"Sounds delicious. What kind?" he asked.

"Chocolate chip! And tonight we're having a sleepover party. I've never had a sleepover before!" Kylee's little cheeks were pink with pleasure.

Tara smiled. "I'm so glad you're having fun with Amanda."

"We're going to the park."

"Nice. You be good and listen to Amanda, okay?"

"Okay, Mommy. When are you coming home?"

"Tomorrow. Amanda will be with you until I get there."

"Okay. Bye." Kylee handed the phone back to Amanda and Rick hung up.

"Feel better?" Rick squeezed her shoulder.

"Yes. Thanks." Tara gave him a smile that made his heart beat a little faster in his chest.

Rick stood and helped Tara off the plane. A chauffer opened the door to a limo and Rick motioned for Tara to slide in first. He joined her and they took off for the theater. Thirty minutes later they arrived.

The chauffer drove slowly, waiting in a line. When it was their turn to get out, the driver hopped out and opened the door. Rick stepped onto the sidewalk and reached out to Tara.

He slid his arm around her as they walked along the red carpet, cameras flashing and reporters calling out questions.

"Rick, when is the wedding?"

"Can we see the ring?"

"Where are you going to get married?"

Rick smiled and pulled Tara closer. "We haven't picked a date yet. Everything is still in the planning stages. I'm just happy she was sober enough to say yes."

He'd meant it as a joke, but Tara's face drained of color, and her smile turned stiff.

He waved at the crowd. "Thank you for your well wishes." He ushered Tara into the building.

She turned to look up at him, a frown pinching her lips together. "Classy."

"I was joking."

"With the way the proposal went down, we probably shouldn't bring attention to it." She pulled away from him and walked into the second set of doors.

She was right. He rushed to catch up to her. "I'm sorry," he whispered. She nodded politely and kept going.

Nice. Now she was mad. He should have kept his big mouth shut. Rick tried to catch up to her and act like nothing was wrong as they made their way into the pre-screening gathering. He put his hand on her back and she gave him a frosty nod.

"Well, look who's here."

Rick knew that voice, and he cringed before he turned around to smile at Vikki Castle. Her platinum blonde hair fell to her shoulders. Ruby red lips pouted at him. Rick braced himself. "Hello, Vikki."

Tara turned to see who he was talking to.

Vikki grinned and grabbed his arm, practically purring. "I didn't know you were going to be here. What a treat. We should do something after this. What hotel are you staying at?"

A startled look came over Tara's face.

Rick wiggled out of Vikki's grasp. "I'm sorry, Vikki, you must not have heard. I'm getting married. This is my fiancée, Tara McDermott. Tara, Vikki Castle. We worked on a film together."

Tara stuck out her hand, and Vikki stared at it like it was covered in pig's blood. Vikki didn't say anything to Tara, just turned back to Rick. "You're not seriously marrying the maid, are you?"

So she *had* heard about his engagement. Rick wanted to strangle her. He desperately wanted to put her in her place, but he knew the rules of the game. You gritted your teeth and didn't tick off people who had influence, like Vikki Castle. "Tara and I are in love."

Vikki's grin turned vicious. "How . . . sweet." She looked down her nose at Tara. "You're so daring, wearing that. I wouldn't be caught dead wearing retail to an event like this."

Tara's cheeks flushed pink and Rick took a protective step toward Tara. "Why don't you go harass someone else?"

"Let's just cut through the bull. I know something's up. You and this . . ." Vikki sneered at Tara, "thing . . . you're not really dating. You don't go for the hometown girls. You're not the relationship type. And when I find out what's up, I'm going to tell all the newspapers."

Rick swallowed hard and tugged at his collar. How could Vikki know they were a fake couple? Was it that obvious? What if she really did find out it was a farce and told the media? He hid the fact that she'd gotten under his skin with sarcasm. "What is this, 1985? Who reads newspapers anymore?"

Vikki's face turned red. "You don't want to mess with me, Rick. That's career suicide."

He took a step back and put his arm around Tara, forcing a smile. "Nice to see you again, Vikki. Tara and I hope you find the happiness we have." He ushered Tara in the other direction.

When they were out of earshot, Tara gripped his arm tightly. "She knows. How can that be?" Her face turned white.

He patted her hand, trying to calm her down. "She knows nothing. Vikki's been trying to get her hooks in me. Maybe she thinks it would help her reputation, or get her a better role, I don't know." He glanced behind them to make sure Vikki hadn't followed them. "But honestly, she's just a big wind bag. Ignore her."

Tara clenched his arm tighter. "Are you sure?"

He wasn't, but he didn't want to admit it. "Yes. She's nothing to worry about."

"Hey, there you two are." Phil clapped him on the back. "How was the flight?"

"Fine," Tara said, biting her lip, her gaze breaking to look over at Vikki.

"What's wrong?" Phil asked.

Great. Now he had to tell Phil about Vikki. That was the last thing he wanted to do. Phil would freak.

Tara leaned closer. "Vikki Castle is stirring up trouble."

"What kind of trouble?"

A waiter in a tux stopped by Phil. He lowered a tray with meats, cheeses, and olives. "Would you care for some?"

Phil picked up a toothpick with a roll of meat coiled on it. "Thanks."

After the server left, Rick stepped closer to answer Phil's question. "She's threatening to tell the press we're not in a real relationship."

Phil choked. "What?" He coughed and pounded on his chest with his fist. "How did she find out?"

"She didn't," Rick said. "She's just digging for something to hang me with."

Phil frowned and Rick could see the thoughts swirling around in his head.

Tara shot a worried glance toward Vikki, who was now chatting with the cast of the movie. "What proof could Vikki dig up? Is it possible she could find the contracts?"

"They're under lock and key at the house," Rick said. "She can't prove anything."

"No." Phil scrubbed a hand over his chin. "But she can make waves and we don't want that. It's good you're here. Mingle, but I also want you to spend time looking completely in love. Make out in front of everyone if you have to. People here need to see that you're crazy about each other."

Tara's eyes widened for a brief moment before she nodded. Rick cleared his throat. "Alright. I'll make it look good."

Phil squeezed his shoulder. "The more people who see you two together, the more it will just become commonplace. Sorry, but you might have to be seen out in public more than we originally thought."

Rick looked to Tara, who was now staring at the floor. She met his gaze and he could see the hesitation in her eyes.

"Only if Tara is okay with it," Rick said.

Tara straightened her back. "Of course."

Phil plucked a glass of wine from a server passing by. Rick reached up and Phil shot him a warning frown. He put his hand down. Maybe when Phil wasn't looking he'd sneak one. A glass of wine wasn't going to make him drunk.

"Catch you two love birds later," Phil said as the crowd of people pressed closer.

After Phil left, Rick put his arm around Tara and pulled her off to the side of the room. He gazed into her eyes, and she smiled tentatively at him.

"Guess we need to make out." He ran his fingers up her arm.

She looked to the floor, but a smile formed on her lips. "It's part of the job."

He hooked his finger under her chin and raised it until she looked into his eyes. "But I don't want to force you to do anything you're uncomfortable with."

She took his hand and ran her thumb over his fingers. "Just kiss me," she said, her smile widening.

He grinned. "Bossy, aren't you?"

Before she could respond, he leaned down and covered her lips with his. The kiss was slow and thorough, and his heart began to race in his chest. He slid his hands around her waist and pulled her closer. Her skin was soft and warm, and he deepened the kiss.

He allowed himself to get lost in the pleasure her lips brought him. She was a different kind of woman than he'd dated in the past. She cared so deeply for her daughter. Maybe that's what made her feel like she had more substance. Deeper feelings than others. He wasn't sure, but he was severely attracted to her, and kissing her was only making it worse.

Chapter 13

ara fought back the urge to pull away from the kiss. It was necessary, she knew, but she was starting to lose herself in Rick, and she knew she couldn't do that. She had to keep her feelings in check. If she allowed herself to fall for him, she'd only end up with a broken heart.

Rick ran his hand up her back, and tingles erupted, making her pulse race. She forced herself to remember this was just an act. Rick wasn't really kissing her. He was playing a part, and she was the female lead. She distanced herself from the kiss, thinking of Kylee and how she would see her tomorrow.

When he pulled back, she smiled at him, hoping it looked realistic. What she wanted to do was run away from him. Go catch her breath in the restroom and gather her wits about her. But instead, she forced herself to melt into his arms.

Rick played with a tendril of her hair. "Think we should mingle?"

"Probably a good idea."

"Maybe in a minute." Rick brushed another light kiss across her lips and tingles shot across her skin. Man, this was going to kill her.

Rick finally pulled back and they walked the room, chatting with the celebrities and producers. She watched as he introduced her to everyone. Tara had to give it to him: he was good at this game. Charm rolled off him in waves. He knew everyone's name and worked the room with ease.

As people started filing into the screening room, Rick took her hand. "Guess we should follow."

She nodded, and they made their way through the doors. Instead of regular theater seats, leather recliners made up the rows of seating. Small tables were spread throughout the room, topped with hors d'oeuvres and wine.

Rick motioned to a couple of seats near a table. "This look okay?"

"Fine." She sat down and nibbled on something wrapped in bacon. It was delicious. Rick grabbed a glass of wine and downed it.

Tara swatted him on the arm. "Stop that."

"Phil worries too much. I'm fine. Wine isn't going to do anything to me."

Tara struggled for a moment between saying something and keeping her mouth shut. She wasn't hired to be his mother. He was a grown man and could make his own decisions. Yet, if he got sloppy drunk and did something else to embarrass himself, it would only reflect poorly on them both. In the end, she decided to shrug and let him drink it. He was right. It was only wine.

She watched the movie and tried to ignore when Rick signaled for more wine throughout the show. Then the party moved to a private home where harder liquor was being served. Tara grabbed Rick's arm the moment he reached for a glass of scotch.

"I'm sorry, I forgot something in the car. Can you come with me?"

Rick slid his arm around her waist. "Of course, baby." He grabbed the glass with his other hand and ushered her out of the room.

"What are you doing?" she hissed. "You can't drink that."

He grinned at her. "Loosen up. It's a party."

"You promised Phil you wouldn't drink."

He chuckled. "Phil went home."

She clenched her hands. "You need to be on your best game."

"It's just one drink. Relax. It's okay." He took a sip.

"You don't make good decisions when you're drinking, and you're going to embarrass me." She gave him what she hoped was a death glare.

He sobered. "I don't want to embarrass you."

"Then put the drink down."

Indecision played across his face, but then he set the glass on a coffee table and straightened. "For you."

Why did that make her heart beat against her rib cage? She took his hands in hers and ignored the warmth as it spread through her. "Thank you."

His hands snaked around her waist. "I won't drink anymore if you lighten up and have some fun."

She stiffened. He kept telling her to loosen up. It was beginning to annoy her. "I can have fun just like the next person."

"Okay, prove it." He tugged her through the house to the open room with the band. People were milling about, mostly talking. He pulled her to him and started swaying with the music.

Heat shot to her cheeks. "No one else is dancing," she whispered.

"That's okay. You don't care, because you're letting loose."

He pushed her back, twirled her, then pulled her to him again. The move made her dizzy and she couldn't help but laugh. "You're crazy."

"I've been called a lot worse." His grin widened as he moved to the music.

She followed his dance steps, keeping up with him. Everyone in the room was now looking at them. Maybe that's what Rick was after. If he wanted people to talk about them, he was sure getting the attention.

Someone whistled after he twirled her a second time, and Tara noticed another couple had joined in the dancing. She couldn't help but smile. Dang, Rick was a good dancer.

The music ended and the band played a slow song. Rick pulled Tara close and her knees went weak. He placed his hand on her upper back, just below her shoulder blade, and took her hand in his. She made the mistake of looking up into his blue eyes. They seemed to hold an unspoken question.

"You look flushed." His voice was low and she leaned forward a little to hear him better.

"You're a good dancer."

"And you're a good kisser."

Heat once again flushed in her cheeks, and Rick seemed to take pleasure in her embarrassment. He smiled and raised one eyebrow. "You're not used to compliments, are you?"

She hadn't really thought about it, but now that Rick brought it up, Bobby hadn't been one to shower her with praise or flattery. He'd been more . . . well, Bobby was all about Bobby. And she'd been fine with that. At least, she'd thought she was. She let his question hang in the air.

His gaze trapped hers. "Let's give them something to remember us by." He dipped her, then held her there as his lips brushed against hers. The kiss was soft, and she didn't have any trouble getting lost in it. When he brought her up, the people in the room cheered.

Tara's heart thumped wildly in her chest. Rick wanted attention, and he'd gotten it. She had to keep reminding herself this was all just for show.

They danced through another song. By the time they left the room, there were a dozen couples dancing. Rick had successfully livened up the party. She picked up a glass of water off the serving table and motioned to the double doors that led outside. "I think I need some air."

Rick nodded and opened the latch, leading her out onto the back deck. The sound of the music faded as they stepped outside. The floral smell of a summer evening wafted in the breeze as twinkle lights suspended above them lit up the area. Tara walked to the railing and looked down. A flower garden stretched out beyond the deck, small lights trailing along a winding path. It took her breath away.

Rick put his hand on her back. "You okay?"

"Yes." She took a long drink of the water. She was fine. At least, that's what she kept telling herself.

"Missing Kylee?"

Guilt surged in her throat. Yeah, that's what she should be upset about, wasn't it? She actually hadn't thought about her much of the evening. Most of her thoughts were centered on how Rick's touch was sending her body into some kind of hyper-alert state. How he smelled like musk and citrus. And then there were the thoughts of his lips on hers.

"Yes," she lied.

"We'll see her tomorrow. In fact, it's almost here." He showed her his watch. Eleven-thirty.

She smiled up at him. He really was a nice guy under the exterior he put on. Why did he have to be so nice? Why did her heart have to speed up like it did? She turned away. "Did you date Vikki Castle? Is that why she's out to get you?" She cringed as soon as the words were out. She hadn't meant to ask that.

Rick shifted his weight. "Didn't date her. More like she came on to me and I said I wasn't interested."

For some reason that made Tara feel better. "She didn't like being rejected."

"No." He turned around to lean against the railing, maybe to see the doors in case anyone snuck out while they were talking. "Vikki's the kind of person who doesn't do anything unless it helps her climb to the top. We were filming a movie together and everyone talked about us being a couple."

He stared at the house, his gaze losing focus. "But being with her was like sitting on nails." He turned to face her, a slight smile on his lips. "Painful and pointless."

Tara laughed. "Don't hide how you feel about her, now. Tell it like it is."

He chuckled. "Enough about Vikki." He put his hands on the railing, one on either side of her. "I don't want to talk about her anymore."

Before Tara could wonder why he was suddenly so close to her, she heard the click of the door and a man and a woman walked out on the deck. Ah, that's why he was making a pass at her. She put her arms around his neck and smiled up at him. "What do you want to talk about?"

"Who said I wanted to talk?" He looked down at her lips.

The couple walked across the deck then down the steps toward the garden. Tara expected Rick to move back, but he stayed where he was. In fact, he pulled her closer, as if he couldn't stop himself.

Tara didn't want to be kissed again by Rick. She was getting too wrapped up in him. Her heart couldn't take any more. So she blurted the first thing she could think of: "Tell me about the girl who broke your heart."

Rick froze, then stiffened and stepped away from her. He worked his jaw. Finally, he turned toward the house. "We should go inside."

She grabbed his arm, stopping him. "I'm sorry."

He shrugged, and she could see he'd thrown up his invisible walls. "Don't worry about it."

"You don't have to tell me about her. But I want you to know I'm a good listener if you ever want to talk."

Rick studied her in the moonlight. His features softened. "It's complicated."

"I'm not going anywhere."

He sighed and broke his gaze, looking out over the grounds. "We were young."

Tara waited for him to continue, folding her arms against the cool breeze.

Rick shrugged out of his jacket. "Here." He helped her slip it on.

"Thanks." The smell of Rick enveloped her and she shivered.

Rick walked over to the railing and gripped the wood, his knuckles white. "Her name was Scarlett. She was my best friend. We grew up together on the road. Our parents were in the same theater group."

"Was she an actress as well?"

He shook his head. "No. She didn't want anything to do with it. Hated not having a permanent home."

Tara nodded and stepped closer to him. When he didn't say anything else, she decided to give him a nudge. "How long did you date her?"

"Five years."

"That's a long time."

"We were going to get married," he said, his voice quiet, his gaze avoiding hers. The pain in his face was clear.

"What happened?"

He pressed his lips together, then stepped away from her, hardening his features. "We didn't." The look in his eyes said he was done talking about it. "Ready to go in?"

She wrapped her arms around her middle. "Yes."

Chapter 14

ick tugged at his collar. How did she do that? Turn it around so he was talking about Scarlett? He didn't want to tell Tara about it. He'd rather forget that part of his past. It didn't make him look good. It would reveal a piece of himself he'd rather keep buried.

Tara slipped off his jacket and handed it back to him. "Thank you."

"No problem." He slung his coat over his shoulder and took her arm. "Are you ready to leave?"

She nodded. They were making their way through the crowd when someone called out, "Hey, Rick! Is that you?"

Rick turned to see Jake Oliver. They'd worked on two different movies together. He looked like a body builder and always got the dumb jock parts. Rick stuck out his hand. "Hey, Jake. How are you?"

"Good. I hear you're getting married? When's the big day?" Jake slung an arm over Rick's shoulders. He smelled of alcohol.

Vikki Castle turned toward them from across the room. "Yes, Rick. When's the wedding?" Her loud voice carried, and people stopped their conversations to look at her.

Tara's eyes grew wide and Rick knew he had to take control of the situation, and fast. "We haven't set a date yet. We're taking things slow."

"Why is that?" Vikki called. She took a step toward them and stumbled a little, her red stilettos wobbling. "You worried you'll change your mind?"

A small crowd of people was forming around them, and panic struck Rick in his chest. What was Vikki doing? She was going to embarrass Tara, and he couldn't have that. "You're drunk, Vikki."

"That never stopped you, Rick." Vikki grinned as the crowd laughed.

Jake chuckled and slapped Rick on the shoulder. "I saw your proposal on YouTube. She's not trapping you into anything, is she?"

"What? No." Rick stepped away from Jack. Is that what everyone thought? She was holding him to a drunk proposal? "I can't wait to marry her."

Vikki's grin turned sour. "Then you should just do it. We are in Vegas after all." This brought a new round of laughter from the crowd.

Sweat broke out on Rick's forehead. They wanted him to marry her tonight? What if he did? Rick looked at Tara, her body was stiff, her face a mask of stone. What if he didn't?

"Do it!" someone yelled.

People started clapping and hollering. "Marry her!"

"What's the matter, Rick?" Vikki said, raising her hands. "You look a little nervous. Are you not really in love?"

This was ridiculous. If they wanted him to prove something, why shouldn't they just go get married? That was the plan anyway. He slid his arm around Tara's waist. "I think eloping is a great idea."

Tara's face drained of color. "You do?" she whispered.

"Why not? We're crazy in love. Let's just do it."

The crowd cheered and Rick pulled Tara to the door. "We'll continue this party at the Chapel-O-Love! Drinks on me."

***

Tara wanted to sink into the floor. What was Rick doing? He wasn't even drunk this time. Why was he letting Vikki's goading get to him?

Heat assaulted her face as Rick ushered her outside. The driver came around the car and opened her door for her. His white-tipped hair caught her attention. His nametag read Liam. "Take us to the Chapel-O-Love," Rick said, grinning and patting Liam's shoulder.

"Yes, sir."

After the limo pulled away from the curb, she turned to him. "What do you think you're doing? This wasn't part of the plan. Phil is going to have a heart attack. We can't elope at a Las Vegas Marry-a-thon!" Her voice rose in pitch with every word she said.

Rick put his palms up. "Whoa, slow down. This isn't a big deal."

"Of course it's a big deal! Do you know what this is going to look like to the world?" Tara clenched her hands, trying to get them to stop shaking.

Rick grinned. "Like we can't keep our hands off each other?"

She gave him her best death-stare. "Is everything a joke to you?"

He sobered. "No. But this isn't worth fighting over."

Tara took in a breath and tried to calm herself. "You are embarrassing me again."

"You're embarrassed because you've slipped out of your role." Rick gently picked up her hands in his. "Close your eyes."

She was too mad to do what he said. She gave him a flat look.

"Seriously. Just do it."

She sighed. "Alright." She closed her eyes.

"Imagine you've found your soul mate. You're giddy in love." As he spoke, he stroked her hands, which sent crazy tingles through her. It was making it hard to concentrate, especially in conjunction with his low, masculine voice and his intoxicating smell. "Everything you do is about how much you love him. You can't get enough. You eat, sleep, and breathe him."

She almost pulled her hands away, but at the last second he stopped stroking and just held them. "There isn't enough time in the day to spend with him. Your pulse races at the sound of his voice. His touch sends your heart into overdrive."

Was he reading her mind? "I get it," she blurted. Her voice sounded a bit too breathy for her liking.

"Take this image and apply it to yourself. You are the one crazy in love." His breath brushed her cheek and she realized he was close enough to kiss her. "With me."

Her eyes flew open and his intense gaze met hers. His eyes were like a glassy lake on a summer day, and she felt like he could see into her depths. She broke his gaze and leaned away from him. "I think I can see it."

"Then running to the chapel tonight isn't unimaginable, is it?" He began stroking her hands again, and she pulled them away, her breathing too out of control.

"I suppose not."

"Okay. So, all you have to do is pretend you are the woman you imagined." He grinned at her, and her heart dropped to her toes.

She plastered on a smile. "All right."

They arrived at the Chapel-O-Love. Liam grinned as they climbed out of the limo. "I'll wait here for you," he said. He looked like he was enjoying a secret.

Rick opened the door for her. He approached the attendant and spoke with her while various famous people milled about in the waiting area. Needless to say, they were delighted to accommodate Rick, even on such short notice.

Before she knew it, Tara was standing at the altar clad in white, her throat tight. She gripped the plastic bouquet of flowers and wondered if she'd leave finger marks on the stem. The words 'giddy in love' rang through her mind as she smiled and tried to act appropriately.

Paparazzi lined the back wall, camera flashes going off. Tara ignored them and continued to smile like she'd won the lottery.

Rick's gaze met hers, and all thought left her brain. Dang, did he get hotter in the last few seconds? What had he done? She couldn't pinpoint it, but he looked different somehow.

The minister began. "We are gathered here—"

Darth Vader's march rang out and the audience burst out laughing. Rick patted his pockets until he brought out his cell phone. "Sorry!" He cut the music off, then he held up the phone and grinned. "You can continue."

The minister spoke, but the words didn't stay in Tara's mind. She was really getting married. For the second time. To an actor. Her throat squeezed tight, constricting her airflow. Why was she doing this? For money? She should know better. This was such a dumb idea.

They said their "I do's" and Rick kissed her. Then it was over and she was throwing her bouquet as rice pelted her. A middle-aged lady snapped a few photos and they were ushered in the back to finish signing papers.

Rick slid his hand around her shoulders. "Well, Mrs. Shade, what do you think? Ready for your honeymoon?"

Honeymoon? What about Kylee? She promised her she'd be home tomorrow. Panic gripped her chest and she struggled for words. "What?" she managed to squeak out.

He glanced in the direction of the paparazzi and celebrities in the other room. "You know, dear. Honeymoon." He wiggled his eyebrows up and down, and the lady behind the desk giggled. Tara was stuck. She couldn't protest in front of anyone.

They finished signing papers, and Tara changed back into her cocktail dress. Were they really going to fly off to some island somewhere, leaving Kylee with the babysitter? She needed to get Rick alone so she could talk to him.

Once they were in the limo, and Rick had spoken to Liam, she rounded on him. "Where are we going? How long will we be there? What about Kylee?"

Rick put his hands on her shoulders. "Hey, chill out. We have to run off on a honeymoon or it will look odd. I'll fly Kylee and Amanda out to us. Amanda can watch Kylee while we are seen in public. The rest of the time it will just be like you're on vacation." His thumbs brushed her skin and she suddenly had a hard time breathing.

Rick continued. "We'll have to go out in public a little so the paparazzi can take photos, but the rest of the time you can just relax on the beach and spend time with your daughter."

Tara took a deep breath. That didn't sound so bad. Taking a vacation with Kylee would be nice. She willed herself to relax and not worry about it. Rick sounded like he had everything under control.

"I own a little place on the secluded island of Lana'i. I'll call and have it set up. We can be there by morning." He pulled out his phone and frowned. "Crud. Phil's been calling."

Tara held her breath as Rick punched in Phil's number. "Hey," he said, like nothing important was going on.

Phil's voice came through the line, hollering. "What did you do?"

Rick made a face and pulled the phone away from his ear. Phil continued to shriek. "I can't leave you alone for one minute. Why did you run off to a Vegas chapel? Have you been drinking? Please tell me you're not drunk."

Rick scowled. "I'm not drunk."

"Then why did you elope? We had this all planned! You've ruined everything!"

"I've got it covered. We were forced into the situation."

Phil lowered his voice so Tara couldn't hear him anymore, but she watched Rick nod. "Yes. It was Vikki."

Tara glanced out the window as they sped down the highway. Nothing had gone as planned. Would Phil wash his hands of the whole thing?

Rick kept speaking, his voice calm. "It's okay, this doesn't mess up our plan. No one knows we're just doing this for publicity. We're still on track. Everything will be fine."

When he hung up, Tara raised an eyebrow. "What did Phil say?"

"He agrees that we did the right thing based on the circumstances."

"Wow, you got him to agree with you?"

He poked her in the side. "Don't act so shocked. Sometimes I do make sense."

Yes. Sometimes. And other times he just had a way of talking people into doing crazy things. Like this whole insane plan. Rick made it seem so logical. But in reality, she was making wild choices and acting like she never would have if she had her head on straight.

She'd better watch it, or she'd end up doing something even worse. Like fall in love with Rick Shade.

Chapter 15

ick spent the rest of the drive on the phone, getting things ready for their last-minute honeymoon. After he and Tara boarded his plane, he finally felt like he could relax. He changed out of his dress clothes into a t-shirt and his favorite lounge pants.

When he saw Tara on the couch, still wearing her dress, her eyes closed, he sat next to her and nudged her awake. "Go change. You can sleep in the bed. I'll take the couch. We'll be taking off soon."

She opened one eye. "You have a bed on your plane?"

He chuckled. "Of course." He motioned to the back of the plane. "Go get some sleep. We'll be flying all night."

"You don't have to tell me twice," she mumbled and picked up her carry-on, then disappeared into the other room.

Rick put his feet up on the coffee table and made himself comfortable. Soon he'd be at his cabin on the beach in Lana'i. He and Tara. His thoughts immediately trained on her. Why was he drawn to her? If it was just physical attraction, he could handle it. He worked around beautiful women all the time. But it was something more. She was beginning to mean something more to him. And he wasn't sure what he was going to do about it.

He sighed and settled into the couch. Tara was too sweet, too trusting. He couldn't let her get too close to him. He wasn't the kind of man who could be with Tara. She'd get hurt in the end. That's what he did. It was in his nature. He couldn't help it. He wasn't a family man.

He drifted off to sleep. When the captain came on to tell them the plane was landing, he stretched and checked the time. It was around eight o'clock in the morning, Hawaii time. He had serious jet lag. Maybe he could nap this afternoon.

Tara came out of the bedroom wearing sweats and a tank top. Her hair was sticking out in all directions, and he hid a smile. "Morning, sunshine."

She gave him a sleepy smile and sat next to him, her hands raised up. "Don't look at me. I'm atrocious."

That wasn't the word he was thinking. He chuckled. "We'll have a car waiting for us when we land."

She buckled her seatbelt and leaned her head against the back of the couch. "Good. I need a shower."

Tara would be happy; there was no staff at his cabin. Just Kanye, and he was only hired to stock the fridge and drive them to and from the airport. She'd be able to make all the sandwiches she wanted.

The airplane landed and they climbed down the steps to the asphalt. Kanye pulled up in his jeep. "Hey, Mr. Shade. It's been a while."

Kanye sported the darkened skin of a native to the islands, and wore cut-off jeans and a muscle shirt. He hopped out of the jeep and grabbed their luggage. "I hear congratulations are in order."

"This is my wife, Tara. Tara, this is Kanye."

Tara shook his hand and smiled. "Nice to meet you."

Kanye opened the passenger door for Tara and helped her in.

Rick climbed in back. He worried a little that Tara would think his cabin was too small. It only had three bedrooms, a small living room area, a kitchen, and an enclosed patio. The one bathroom had a shower, but no tub.

As they drove, Tara pointed out the landscaping. "What are these bright purple flowers? They're everywhere."

"They're bougainvillea," Kanye answered.

"They're beautiful. I can smell them in the air." She continued to marvel at the view as they made their way down the road.

They pulled up in front of the cabin. His car sat under the car port. He'd had Kanye gas it up before they arrived. Rick hopped out and unlocked the front door, letting Tara enter first. He suddenly wished he'd paid to renovate the place, like he'd always had in mind. The hardwood floors were old and scarred, and the wood paneling made the place look so dated.

"It needs updating," Rick said.

Tara turned to him, a bright smile on her face. "It's perfect."

"Really?" He looked around the living room. "It's not too small?"

Tara walked over to the stairs that led to the upstairs bedrooms. "No, it's great. Mind if I check it out?"

"Be my guest."

Kanye walked in and set the luggage down. He grinned at Rick and slapped him on the back. "Enjoy your stay." He ducked back out before Rick had a chance to say anything else.

Rick peered out the window and watched the jeep take off down the road. Tara came to the railing upstairs. "This is great. There's so much character."

"I bought it for the view out back."

Tara came down the steps. "Can I see?"

"Sure. There's a small deck, and a trail that leads down to the beach."

Tara walked through the enclosed patio and opened the back door. She gasped. "Rick. This is heaven."

He smiled to himself. The cabin wasn't much, but the backyard was spectacular. "I like to sit out here and watch the sun set."

Tara walked to the edge of the deck and put her hand up to shield the sun from her eyes. "What's that bit of white down there in the trees?"

"A hammock."

"Are you kidding me? I can't wait to try it out. This is so peaceful here."

He was thrilled she liked the place. "It is."

She turned back toward the cabin. "I'm in desperate need of a shower. Do you mind?"

"Go ahead."

"Thanks." She headed toward the door.

"If you want to make a list of items you need from the store, I'll text it to Kanye."

Tara's steps slowed. "Why don't we run to the store together after I shower?"

"Yes. That's fine. We can go after you clean up." He'd just put on a baseball cap. Most of the time that worked, and no one recognized him.

Rick changed into one of the outfits he had in his closet, and left the scruff on his face. While Tara showered, he scrounged around in the kitchen. By the time she was done, he'd cut up some fresh fruit and had the yogurt dip open and ready.

Tara came in the room, her phone pressed to her ear. She had her hair pulled up again, and he wished she'd left it down. "Did you have a good sleepover, sweetie?" She pointed to the spread of fruit and gave Rick a thumbs up.

He motioned for her to sit down and eat with him.

170

"Which movie did you watch? That one, again?" She mouthed, 'Poor Amanda.'

Rick popped a grape in his mouth and took a second to admire Tara's sundress. It had little purple flowers on it, and it hugged her curves.

She finished up her phone call with Kylee, then hung up and set her phone on the table. Her gaze traveled over him. "What are you wearing?"

"What?"

"You look like a tourist."

"I'll blend in."

She bit into a strawberry, not quite hiding her smile. "Okay."

"You don't like the flowered shirt?"

"It's . . . bright." She turned away from him, and he had a sneaking suspicion she was laughing at him.

"I'll have you know, the flowered look is very popular here." He said it with a straight face, but he couldn't help the smile in his voice.

"Really?" She turned back around. "Well, I won't lose you in a crowd, that's for sure."

He laughed. "Want me to change?"

"No way. I want to see you out in public like that."

Almost without thinking about it, he swiped his finger into the fruit dip and wiped it on her nose.

She jerked back and her mouth fell open, a gasp escaping. "Oh, no. Now you've done it." She dipped her finger in and he hopped off his chair before she could come at him with it.

She leaped forward, but he was too fast and moved out of the way before she reached him. He sidestepped around the table, toward the sink. She came at him again, this time successfully smearing dip on his nose.

He grabbed her wrists while she laughed at him. "I'm funny, huh?" he asked, out of breath from goofing around.

"You sure look funny to me." She grinned at him.

He stared into her eyes, and suddenly the mood shifted. His gaze traveled down to her lips. What would she do if he kissed her? Would she stop him? Or would she allow it? It seemed as if he had no willpower to stop himself. He slowly moved closer to her.

Her phone chimed and broke the spell. He let go of her hands and wiped the yogurt dip off his face. Tara turned around and grabbed her phone off the table. She stared at the screen.

"It's Bobby."

He picked up a napkin and handed it to her. "You've still got . . ." He motioned to his nose.

She wiped it off.

"What does he want?"

She closed her eyes and shook her head. "He's mad. Said something about us not holding up our end of the deal."

"What? Give me that."

Tara seemed surprised, but she handed her phone over to him. He read the text.

I don't like being played a fool. Your husband better hold up his end of the bargain or I'll become the nuisance you don't want.

There it is. A threat in print. But was it enough to issue a restraining order? Rick doubted it. Threatening to be a nuisance isn't much. Rick typed in a response.

This is Rick. I did what you asked. Now leave us alone.

His response came back quickly.

Your agent told me to take a flying leap.

Rick swiped his hand over his face. Crud. He'd told his agent to call. He didn't specify what he wanted his agent to do.

I'll talk to him.

You'd better. I don't like being jerked around.

Rick wanted to answer with something about being a jerk, but forced himself to calm down.

I'm on my honeymoon. I'll talk with him as soon as I can.

Maybe that would buy him some time.

Bobby answered back. *Oh, yeah. Congratulations.*

Rick changed the screen and handed the phone back to Tara. "I took care of it."

She eyed him skeptically. "What did you do?"

He sighed. "I told him I'd talk to my agent."

"Wait, you're trying to help Bobby?"

Rick folded his arms. "No. I'm trying to appease Bobby. We can't get a restraining order until he hurts one of us, and I'd rather not have that happen."

She seemed to take in what he said, then nodded. "You're right. I don't want to risk anything happening to Kylee."

"Me neither." He motioned to the table. "Are you done eating?"

"Yes, I am, Magnum P.I. Let's go shopping." She tossed him a snarky grin and put the lid on the yogurt.

He wanted to swat her behind, but kept his hands to himself. "Whatever. I'm cool and you just can't stand it."

Her laughter bounced off the walls, and he couldn't stop himself from grinning.

Chapter 16

ara pulled a gray button-up shirt from the hanger and tossed it to Rick. The store actually had a decent selection. "Here you go. For when you want to be done looking like you lost a bet."

"Ouch!" He held the shirt to his chest, looking in the mirror. "You're starting to hurt my ego."

She giggled and slapped him on the back. "And I thought nothing could hurt your ego."

He turned quickly and snaked his arm around her waist, pulling her to him. "Woman, you're driving me crazy."

Tara's heart raced in her chest. She knew he was just flirting because they were in public, and they had to act like a couple in love, but the way he was looking at her felt real. The whole thing felt . . . different than she thought it would.

His gaze fell to her lips and he leaned down, close enough that she could easily close the distance. "I'm going to kiss you now," he said, his voice low enough that no one else could hear it.

Her mouth grew dry. It was all for show, but she almost didn't care anymore. She wanted him to kiss her. "Okay," she whispered.

The kiss took her breath away. The way her heart beat against his chest, and how her lips tingled as he teased them with his own, she almost melted into the floor. Was this what it was like, when two people loved each other?

She froze. Where had that come from? She wasn't in love with Rick. Was she?

He pulled away and looked at her, an unspoken question in his eyes. She slapped on a fake grin. "You'd better get more than one shirt if your closet is full of 'Grandpa on a cruise' outfits."

He smiled, but she could see the reservation hidden behind his eyes. "You got it."

Patting the back of her head, she made sure her hair wasn't falling out of her bun. She peered at their cart and assessed the assortment of clothes she'd picked out. They should last her for the two weeks they were planning on 'honeymooning.' "I'll go grab the personal items I'll need. Meet you at the register in ten minutes?"

He nodded.

She practically ran to get out from under his scrutiny. What was she all upset about? She wasn't in love with Rick. That was preposterous. She signed up for kisses in public and dancing at parties. There was no way she'd let his pretty face get to her. She wasn't anything more than the hired help. And he was just a handsome man.

Okay. A drop-dead gorgeous movie star. There. She admitted it. But that didn't mean she was in love with him.

By the time she'd gathered up a toothbrush, shower gel, and her favorite disposable razor, she'd convinced herself she was being paranoid. Stepping away from his charm had put her head on straight. She didn't act for a living, so maybe she'd allowed herself to get into the role a bit more than career actors. But now she knew. She just had to keep reminding herself that this was her job for the next year.

And that worked great until she had to stand next to him at the register and smell his fresh, masculine scent. She bit her bottom lip and folded her arms tight. This was going to be one long year.

They paid for their purchases and she climbed into the jeep. Rick gripped the top of the steering wheel with one hand and looked over at her. "Do you want to see more of the island?"

She leaned her head back on the headrest. "Maybe later. Right now I'm thinking a nap in your hammock sounds like heaven."

He cocked his head at her, a slight smile on his face. "Sure."

She closed her eyes as they drove to the cabin. The smell of the ocean was relaxing. After they took their things into the house, Rick opened the back door and motioned for her to go.

He followed her outside. She peered at him, wondering why he was following her, but didn't want to be rude. They walked down the path toward the hammock. "This is lovely," she said as they approached the beach.

He shoved his hands in his pockets. "I love how quiet it is here. L.A. is great, but here I can rejuvenate."

The hammock stretched between two palm trees right before the grass turned to sand. Tara shielded her eyes and looked out at the ocean. "I can see why."

"The beaches in L.A. are always so crowded. When I come here, I can clear my head and think."

Tara nodded, then looked down at the hammock. "How do I get in this?"

Rick slid his hands over her hips. "Move closer."

She stepped toward the suspended fabric, ignoring how his hands made electricity shoot through her. "Okay."

"Straddle the hammock, then slowly sit down."

She did as he said, but wobbled. "Whoa, I feel like I'm going to fall out."

"Steady. Just don't lean too far one way or the other. You kind of have to balance in it for a second, then lean back and lift your feet in."

She looked up at him skeptically. "Sure, easy for you to say. You're standing on solid ground. This thing doesn't feel too steady."

He chuckled and took her hand. "Come on. Lean back."

"Alright, alright." She sank into the hammock. "You're right, it's better when I'm farther in."

"Now just pick up your feet and put them in."

She tested the waters with one foot, then lifted the second one. "Ha, I did it."

He let go of her hand and sat on the ground next to her. "Perfect."

She peeked over at him, careful not to lean too much and spill out. "What are you going to do? Nap in the grass?"

"Do you mind?" He stretched out and crossed his ankles. His muscles flexed as he adjusted his hat so the bill covered his face.

She didn't want to tell him she doubted she could rest with him so close. His smell wafted up in the breeze and solidified her thoughts. Her insides tied up in knots. She exhaled and closed her eyes. "I don't mind."

He didn't say anything else, and she tried to listen to the sound of the waves on the beach instead of imagining snuggling with Rick in the hammock. She could do this. She could get over her—whatever it was she had for Rick—and behave like a normal person around him. And she should be able to fall asleep, because she was definitely tired.

Birds chirped while the breeze gently rocked her, and her brain ticked off all the reasons she and Rick would be good together. They had plenty of attraction. Her skin sizzled, even now, and he wasn't even touching her. Just lying on the grass near her. He made her smile. He was kind.

And why was she listing out all of his good qualities instead of sleeping? She took in a deep breath and let it out slowly.

"Can I ask you something?"

His deep voice startled her. She thought he'd fallen asleep. "Sure."

"You said you wanted to move to Iowa to raise Kylee. Is it really because the values and the people there are so different? Or is it because you want to take her far away from Bobby?"

Ouch. What a question. She wrestled with how to answer it. Was she really taking Kylee to Iowa to hide from her ex?

"Sorry," he said. "That kind of came out wrong. I didn't mean to offend you."

"No, you didn't offend. I really thought I was doing it for the values, but you make a good point. Maybe part of me is trying to shield her from her father."

"I don't blame you. He's a jerk."

"He is."

"If he weren't in the picture, would you consider living in L.A.?"

Why was he asking this? She couldn't imagine staying in a city that only reminded her of her own folly. "No." Unless he was asking because he wanted her to stay . . .

"Not that I'm trying to persuade you or anything. Just trying to understand your motivations."

Sure. Of course. She shouldn't be thinking about them as a couple anyway. They were no such thing. "Right."

They were silent for a few moments before Tara got up the courage to speak. "I guess my motivations are complicated. I want Kylee to be loved by those around her. Growing up in Iowa, I always felt like I had a community of people who I could turn to if I were in trouble."

"That's nice. I kind of had the same thing, only with the theater people we traveled with. We were a close-knit group."

"Yes. Right now I feel like it's just me and Kylee against the world. I want to go somewhere where she can have that feeling of family."

"Where in Iowa would you move?" He threaded his fingers behind his head and looked at her.

"I've always liked Ames."

"Is that where your parents live?"

"No. They live in Iowa Falls." She stared up at the wispy clouds, hoping he wouldn't ask.

"Why wouldn't you want to move to Iowa Falls, then?"

He asked. She sighed and shifted to get more comfortable. "My father disowned me when I married Bobby." The words brought up all the pain and suffering from the past. The yelling. Her father telling her never to speak to him again.

"Why?"

"He thought we were too young. The ironic thing is, his attitude just pushed me to marry faster, instead of making me come to my senses. He was right. We were too young." She swallowed back the hurt. She'd made the best of the situation.

"What about your mom?"

More pain swelled in her chest. "We haven't spoken since that day. Casualty of war I suppose."

Rick adjusted his cap and looked at her. "How can a parent disown a child for making a choice? That's just going to push them away."

"My thoughts exactly. I may not always like what Kylee wants to do, but I will never shove her away. I know how that feels."

"My father never disowned me, but I had a similar experience when I decided to go into screen acting."

"Why did he have a problem with that?"

"He said it was beneath me. Stage acting is art, at least in his eyes. Making movies is selling out."

Tara looked over at him. "That's hogwash. I've seen what you can do. It takes a lot of talent."

He grinned at her. "Are you calling me talented?"

"Don't get all egotistical on me." She rolled her eyes.

He squinted. "You've got something on your face." He motioned to her cheek.

She swiped her hand over her skin. "Did I get it?"

"No, it's still there." He reached up, as if to wipe it off, but his hand wasn't close enough. "I can't reach."

She leaned closer and suddenly the hammock twisted and threw her off balance. It flipped and she landed on top of Rick. "Oh!"

His laugh echoed through the palm trees. She tried to roll off him but his arms held her tight. She shoved his shoulder. "You did that on purpose."

"Of course I did." His smile crinkled the skin around his eyes.

A few strands of hair had come loose, and they hung down as she stared at him. He slowly reached up and removed the clip that held her hair up. It spilled down over her shoulders.

"There," he said quietly. "I've been wanting to do that."

She slid off and lay in the grass beside him, gazing up, her heart beating wildly. "Why did you want to do that?"

"Don't know. Just did." He rolled onto his side and leaned on his elbow.

She self-consciously touched her hair. "It's easier to get work done when it's up and out of the way."

He picked up a strand of her hair and fingered it. "I think it looks nice down. Not everything you do has to be practical."

She drew in her courage and gazed into his mesmerizing blue eyes. "Marrying you wasn't practical."

His grin widened. "Now, we've been over this. It was very practical. That's how I convinced you to do it."

He was right. Him and his stupid logic. She was pretty sure he'd somehow charmed her or tricked her in some way. When she was in her right mind, she knew their plan was insane. But when she was around Rick, he did something to her. Messed with her head. "That, and the healthy sum you're paying me."

As soon as the words were out, she regretted them. His smile faded and he nodded, inching away from her. "Yes." He laid back down and put his cap over his eyes. She could feel him withdrawing from her. "The money."

She climbed back into the hammock, careful not to tip it, feeling terrible. Why had she brought up the money? Was it to disguise the fact that she had a crazy crush on him? She closed her eyes, not wanting to think about it anymore. Sleep came to her then, and when she awoke, Rick was gone.

Chapter 17

ick shoveled rice into his mouth, trying to get through the dinner as fast as he could. He'd taken Tara out to a local restaurant, but things had turned quite awkward since she spelled out to him her motivations for being with him. Money. Why had he thought she might actually like him? Maybe because his attraction for her had grown, and he thought she might feel something similar?

Stupid. Why was he doing this to himself? He should know better. He and Scarlett dated before he grew famous. He had known she didn't have ulterior motivations. But after that, he hadn't met anyone simply interested in him. His money or fame was what attracted them now. And he was fine with that, right? It's the life he chose. He just needed to remember: no falling in love. He had flings. He didn't have real relationships.

Tara pushed her food around with her fork.

"Not hungry?" he asked.

"Just worried. I hope Kylee isn't frightened by the plane ride."

Rick glanced at his watch. "They should be arriving in an hour. Would you like me to text the staff to see how things went while we were gone?"

"I'd like that," she said, her shoulders lowering.

"Will do." He reached into his pocket and brought out his phone.

Her gaze softened and she reached across the table to touch his hand. "Thanks."

He pulled away from her touch. "Sure."

She leaned back and studied him. She looked like she was going to speak but changed her mind and lifted her fork to her mouth.

His phone chimed right away. *Everything went smoothly. Kylee was excited to get on the airplane.*

Rick showed the text to Tara, who smiled. "I'm glad she wasn't upset. Thank you for texting."

"No problem."

The waitress stopped by. "How was everything tonight?"

"It was perfect." Tara's smile seemed forced.

The waitress set the check on the table. "You can pay whenever you're ready."

Rick took care of the bill and they left. The night air felt good, the breeze blowing as they bounced along the dirt roads in his car. Tara inhaled. "The air smells so amazing."

"We filmed part of *Extra Curricular* here. I fell in love with it."

"I can see why."

Rick parked the car at the airport. Tara turned to him. "I think I owe you an apology."

He raised his hand. He didn't want any sympathy from her. "No need."

"Yes, I messed things up between us. I didn't mean to imply the only reason I married you was for the money."

A slow anger burned in his gut. "That *is* why you married me, though. Isn't it?"

"It's true, I originally said yes for the money." Her gaze dipped. "But I've gotten to know you since then."

"And now you're in it for my winning personality?" He laughed, but it came out harsh. "Don't try to flatter me. I'm paying you to help my career. Let's not try to pretend it's anything else."

He gripped the steering wheel and scanned the skyline for his jet. Tara pressed her lips together tight. The air between them grew heavy. The seconds ticked by as neither of them spoke.

A few minutes later he spotted the plane. Soon it landed and taxied to their area. The crew pulled the steps down.

Tara got out of the car and waited by the bottom of the stairs. Kylee appeared and Tara's countenance transformed. She smiled and Kylee squealed. "Mommy!"

Amanda held the little girl's hand as she clamored down the steps clutching her Winnie the Pooh bear. Tara crouched down and hugged her daughter.

"I was above the clouds!" Kylee shouted.

"You were? Did it scare you?"

Kylee's nose wrinkled. "It was fun! It made my tummy feel funny. Can I do it again?"

Rick chuckled. "Sure, when we go back to L.A."

"Rick!" Kylee ran to him. He crouched down like he'd seen Tara do. Kylee threw her arms around his neck, so he picked her up. She weighed almost nothing. He felt an urge to protect her, for some strange reason. He held her tight. "Are you my new Daddy?"

He looked at Amanda, who blushed. "Sorry, it was all over the news. She kept asking about it, so I told her you guys got married."

Tara didn't look amused, but she stayed silent. Rick patted Kylee on the back. "Sure, Ladybug. You can call me Daddy if you want to."

Tara's frown deepened, and Rick hoped she wouldn't argue with him in front of Amanda. One of the crew brought Kylee's booster seat out of the plane and Rick buckled it into the back seat. He put the luggage in the back, then climbed in the driver's seat.

"Can you sit by me?" Kylee asked, her large eyes trained on him.

"Rick needs to drive, honey," Tara said climbing in back. "I'll sit beside you." She leaned over and kissed Kylee's forehead.

Amanda took the front passenger seat. After they arrived at the cabin Rick gave Amanda the quick tour.

"Are you guys in the master bedroom on the main floor then?" Amanda asked, picking up her suitcase.

Rick shot a look at Tara, who was frozen, her eyes wide. "Um . . ." She cast him a helpless look.

"Yes, we're in the master bedroom."

Tara's face drained of color. "I actually thought Kylee might need me to sleep with her. Upstairs."

"Nonsense. This is your honeymoon. Kylee and I can have a sleepover. Right, squirt?"

Kylee clapped her hands and ran toward Amanda. "Yay! Can I, Mom? Please?"

Tara stared at him, one last pleading look in her eyes.

"I think that's a great idea," he said.

As soon as Amanda and Kylee disappeared upstairs with their suitcases, Tara rounded on him. "What are you doing?" she hissed.

"Acting like a married couple. We should be more careful now that Vikki's trying to spread rumors. What if she digs around and starts talking to people? Can you imagine what Amanda would tell her if we didn't spend our honeymoon in the same bedroom?"

"This wasn't part of the plan," she whispered.

"Don't worry. I'll take the floor."

"You bet you will." She stormed past him into the bedroom.

***

Rick dressed in his lounge pants and T-shirt and brushed his teeth. He cautiously entered the bedroom in case Tara wasn't done dressing. She was sitting on the bed in a nightgown, brushing her hair. He loved the way it cascaded down her shoulders and fell to the middle of her back. Wait, why was he thinking about her hair? He needed to stop thinking about her at all.

He turned his back on her and grabbed a blanket from the small closet. "Toss one of those pillows to me, would you?"

She picked up the nearest pillow and launched it at his head. He caught it before it hit him. "Testy, aren't you?"

"You do realize you've created a real problem. Once we go back to L.A. I'll have to move into your bedroom or it will look really odd."

He waggled his eyebrows at her. "I don't mind, babe."

She glared at him. "Well, I do."

He exhaled and plopped down on the floor with his blanket. "Fine. I'll think of something."

"Good. Because this is unacceptable."

Unacceptable? Really? He was the one sleeping on the hard floor. He spread the blanket on top of his legs. "Come on. I haven't once tried to get you in my bed."

"And you think I should be thanking you for that?"

He let out a frustrated grunt and laid down. He decided not to answer her, or he might dig himself in deeper. He scrunched the pillow up until it was at least semi-comfortable and closed his eyes.

The lamp clicked off and the room enveloped in darkness. His side began hurting from the pressure of the hard floor so he turned to lay on his back. After a few minutes his back hurt, and he rolled to his other side. This was going to be a long night.

Tara sighed. "I'm sorry. I shouldn't have gotten so mad."

What should he say to that? For some reason, he couldn't think of anything that might not get him into further trouble, so he stayed silent.

The bed rustled. "Rick?" she whispered. "You awake?"

"Yes."

"You still upset with me?"

He was surprised to find all his anger had fizzled. How did she do that? "No."

She was quiet for a few moments before she spoke again. "I feel stupid in this king-sized bed while you sleep on the floor. That can't be comfortable."

He scratched his chin. "What are you saying? You want me in the bed?"

"I overreacted. You were right. You've been a perfect gentleman. If you want to sleep in the bed, I trust you."

"Good, because the floor is making my butt go numb." He climbed onto his side of the bed and fluffed the pillow. "Much better."

In the dim light of the bedroom, he could see Tara looking at him. After a minute, when she didn't look away, he grew curious. "What?" he asked.

"What happened with Scarlett? Why didn't you get married?"

He drew in a deep breath. He shoved his hands under his head and stared up at the ceiling. He might as well tell her. If he didn't answer, Tara would just ask again another time. She should know what kind of a person he truly was. "Scarlett wanted a family."

"Most girls do."

"Yes. But she also wanted a stable husband. Someone who held a boring office job. Clock in at nine, get off at five. Home for the weekends."

Tara slowly nodded. "And you were just getting your acting career started."

"Yes."

"I understand."

He blinked back the emotion swelling in him. "No, I don't think you do. She asked me to leave with her. Go move to somewhere like Iowa and start a family. I thought about it, I really did. But in the end, I chose my acting career over her."

"You wanted to follow your dreams."

He narrowed his eyes, his own self-loathing making him shake. "No. I gave up the woman I loved for money and fame."

Tara was silent, so he continued, making sure she understood what he did. "She gave me a choice . . . and I chose *me*, not her."

"She shouldn't have forced you to choose," Tara said quietly.

"No, she was right. It made me realize I'm not cut out for settling down. I'm too concerned with my own self-interests."

"Rick—"

"Don't you see? I loved her. And I ripped her heart out and sent her packing. All because I wanted to further my career." He didn't mean for his voice to crack, but the image of Scarlett standing outside his apartment, tears streaming down her face, came into his mind and his throat closed. He'd slammed the door in her face. Who does that to the woman they love?

Tara laid her hand on his arm. "You blame yourself."

He jerked away. "Of course I blame myself. Haven't you been listening? I *am* to blame. I loved her and I let her go." All of the feelings he'd been burying over the years surfaced, and he couldn't speak anymore. Guilt and remorse suffocated him.

"She should've supported you in your career choice."

"Like you did with Bobby? Yeah, that sure worked out." He fired the words off like bullets, and regretted it the moment they were out. More guilt surged in him, making it hard to swallow.

He heard the sheets rustle, then silence came, until a soft sob stabbed through his heart. She was crying. And it was his fault. He maneuvered over to her side of the bed and threaded his arm around her stomach, pulling her to his chest. "I'm sorry. I didn't mean it. Please don't cry."

She stayed silent and he buried his face into her bare shoulder. "I'm such a jerk."

She wiped at her eyes and took in a steadying breath. "You lashed out at me because you feel guilty for what happened with Scarlett."

Her words sliced through him, and he realized she was right. "Guilty. Yes." He forced himself to continue. "I hate myself for what I did," he whispered, his gut clenching. He blinked back the emotion.

She rolled over to face him and placed a hand on his cheek. "Don't be so hard on yourself."

"I'm a terrible person."

"No." Tara's thumb caressed his cheek. "You love acting. I've seen it on your face. She didn't truly know you if she thought you'd ever be happy stuck at an office job."

He let her words sink in. She was right yet again. He lived for the thrill of nailing a scene. He loved it when he got so into character that he had a hard time separating himself. It exhilarated him. "How do you do that?"

"What?"

"How do you see me like that?"

She smiled, her eyes glistening. "Like I said. I've gotten to know you."

His gaze landed on her lips. The desire to kiss her hit him in his chest. He pushed the thought from his head. It wouldn't be a good idea to start something like that. Instead, he took her hand in his. "You're a beautiful person."

"You may not realize it yet, but so are you." She kissed the tip of his nose and then rolled away from him. It took all his willpower to move to his side of the bed. He lay on his back and listened to her even breathing until he fell asleep.

Chapter 18

ara woke, not really sure where she was until she spied the empty side of the bed where Rick had slept. She was in Lana'i. On her honeymoon.

Her heart squeezed in her chest as she thought about Rick and what he'd told her. He had let the love of his young life go because their goals weren't the same. She didn't support his career choice. And he'd been beating himself up over it for the last decade.

But what he didn't realize was if she couldn't support him in his choice to be an actor, there would have been many other areas of conflict for them. She wanted to change him, and that never works in a relationship. He blamed himself, but as painful as it was to break up with Scarlett, he would have been miserable staying with her.

Tara slipped out of bed and dressed. A wonderful smell filled the room as she pulled her hair back in a ponytail. Was Rick cooking? She left the bedroom and found him standing at the kitchen stove.

"Hi," she said, suddenly feeling shy around him, but not really understanding why.

He turned to her. "Good morning. No one else was up, so I decided to make breakfast." He motioned to a plate. "Want to butter the toast for me?"

"Sure." She opened the fridge and pulled out the butter. "Did you sleep okay?"

He nodded. "You?"

"Fine." She wasn't going to mention how she dreamed of them dancing, then standing at the alter repeating their wedding vows. In her dream, after the wedding, he picked up Kylee, like he'd done after his jet landed. Kylee was smiling at him, and he looked at her like she was the light of his life. It felt real. Like they were family.

Rick grabbed a couple of plates from the cupboard and scraped the eggs off the frying pan onto the two plates. "Here you go," he said, handing her one.

She buttered the toast and slid one onto his plate. He pulled two forks from the drawer and they sat down. Tara stabbed her eggs and lifted them to her mouth. Hot, fresh, and...crunchy?

She stopped chewing and stared at the eggs. "I think I found a piece of shell," she said, her mouth full of unchewed eggs.

"Oh, sorry, I thought I got all that out of there." He gave her an apologetic smile. He handed her a napkin and she spit out the eggs as discreetly as she could.

The toast couldn't be messed up, so she took a bite of that. A little cold, but better than crunching on eggshells. "No problem." At least he'd tried to cook for them. She was beginning to see the advantages of him hiring a cook.

"Mommy!" Kylee bounded toward her in her pink unicorn pajamas. "I'm hungry."

"I'll make you some eggs," Tara said, scooting her plate back. Maybe she wouldn't offend Rick too badly if she snuck some of them for herself.

She started on the eggs while Rick finished eating his breakfast. Kylee chatted about her time with Amanda and how they played games and watched movies. Amanda entered the room and Tara added two more eggs to the pan.

"Want to go whale watching today?" Rick asked.

205

Kylee squealed. "Whales? I want to see whales!"

"Sounds like fun," Tara said.

While she finished cooking the eggs, Rick washed the dishes. Tara was impressed he didn't just leave the dirty dishes in the sink like he did at home. Maybe with no staff here, he was used to cleaning up after himself. She had to admit, he looked sexy with his sleeves rolled up and his hands in soapy water. His forearms were muscular.

After breakfast, Rick stuck on a pair of sunglasses and they piled in his vehicle to go tour the island. Tara was amazed at how small it was. She could see the ocean from almost anywhere they went. They ended up at a pier, and he paid for a whale watching excursion for the four of them.

When it came time to step on the ramp, Kylee cried and held onto Rick's legs. He picked her up and whispered something in her ear. She settled down and held onto his neck. He stepped onto the boat and took Kylee over to the railing so she could look out at the water.

Tara stood next to him and grabbed the railing. The tour guide spoke for a minute about the island, then started up the engine and they took off.

Rick slid his hand around Tara's waist as they sped out farther into the ocean.

She looked up at him and he smiled down at her. "Thanks for talking to me last night," he said, his voice so low no one else could hear them over the roar of the engine.

What was she to say to that? He had opened up to her, and it had changed something between them. She wasn't exactly sure what yet, but the air between them was different. She wrapped her arm around him and snuggled into his chest. No words would come to her, so she stayed silent.

The boat slowed and the tour guide pointed out where to look and what to look for. He showed them where the binoculars were kept in case they wanted a better look. They sat for a few minutes, with nothing happening before a small mound rose to the surface of the water in the distance. "There," the guide pointed.

A blast of air and water came from the whale, and Kylee giggled, pointing. "Look!"

"That's so cool," Amanda said, picking up a pair of binoculars.

They took turns using the binoculars and watching for more whales. In all, they spotted three before it was time to go back to shore. Kylee clung to Rick the entire time. As they sped back to the dock, Kylee snuggled into his shoulder and he rubbed her back.

Looking at them together nearly broke Tara's heart. Why couldn't Bobby have been that kind of father? Why was Rick taking to the role so perfectly? She pushed the thought out of her head. She didn't want to think of him as playing a role. Now wasn't the time to think about how temporary their situation was. She was having a good day.

They ate at a small seafood place. No one seemed to recognize Rick. Maybe that's why he wore the sunglasses. She watched him as he interacted with Kylee. Her daughter clung to him as she sat on his lap at the restaurant. She refused to try the shrimp until he ate some, then she willingly gobbled up her food.

Near the end of the meal Rick's cell phone rang and he excused himself to take the call. When he came back to the table, his expression was unreadable, and Tara wondered what the call had been about. He didn't say anything, so she left it alone.

They made it back to Rick's cabin in the early afternoon. "Want to go see the beach?" he asked.

Kylee nodded up at him. Tara's heart squeezed to see the admiration in her eyes. "I want to see more whales!"

He chuckled. "We probably won't see more whales at my beach, but we can look for seashells. Would you like that?"

Kylee clapped her hands and ran to the back door. "Yes!"

Amanda followed them down the path to the sand. Kylee giggled and ran to the water's edge. Tara turned to Rick. "Are there undercurrents here?"

"Sometimes. It's best to keep her out of the water."

Tara walked toward Kylee and held out her hand. "Stay with me, okay? This water is for looking at, not swimming in."

Kylee pouted, pulling away from her. "I want Rick."

He walked to them and took Kylee's hand. "Listen to your mom, okay? Let's find some shells."

Tara sat in the sand and watched Amanda, Kylee, and Rick picking up shells and running from the waves as they came in. Soon Rick joined her and it was just Amanda and Kylee playing on the beach.

"Is it always like this?"

She peered at him, not understanding. "What do you mean?"

He gazed out at Kylee, his expression contemplative. "Your daughter. She's adorable. And then she's looking at me with those big eyes and I can't say no to her."

Tara threw her head back and laughed. "Oh, she's got you wrapped around her little finger, doesn't she?"

His eyes crinkled as he gave her a shy smile. "I guess so."

They fell into a companionable silence as they watched Kylee run along the beach, her short legs moving so fast they blurred. Rick looked happy. It seemed different somehow from before. He wasn't as guarded. The air between them grew charged.

He picked up her hand and traced a finger along her skin. "Can I ask you a personal question?"

"Yes."

"Would there ever be a time when you would want to see your father again?"

She eyed him suspiciously. "Why?"

He didn't look up at her, just continued to stare down at her hand, his touch sending little zaps through her. "Maybe Kylee should know her grandparents."

Tara's gut instinct was to pull away, but she forced herself to remain still. Rick didn't know her father. He couldn't know the pain her father caused her the day he forced her out of his life. Tara took a steadying breath. "My father wouldn't want me contacting him. He made that clear."

Rick's gaze connected with hers. "Time can change people. And other things, too."

Something in his eyes made Tara aware that this wasn't just a simple conversation. "What happened?"

He looked down at their hands, still touching. "Your father called."

"What? He called you?" Too many questions swirled around in her head. How did her father get Rick's number? Was that the phone call from earlier? What had he wanted?

"My number isn't published. He called around until he got Phil on the phone."

Her throat constricted. Why was her father trying to get a hold of Rick? Was something wrong? "What did he want?"

"He wants to see Kylee."

Chapter 19

ara's throat closed up. Why would her father even care? She pulled her hand away from Rick. "I don't think that's a good idea."

Rick peered down, a guilty look on his face and his fingers absently drawing in the sand.

"What did you do?"

"I said we'd make a trip out to Iowa." He met her gaze. "I'm sorry. I should have talked to you about it first."

Heat flushed through her. "Yes, you should have. Now you have to call back and tell them we're not going."

He blinked at her. "Look, I know it's none of my business, but just hear me out."

She didn't want to listen. She wanted to punch him. But her rational and less-violent side won out and she nodded.

"Your father had no idea you and Bobby had a baby. When he saw his own granddaughter on television, he was shocked."

A little bit of guilt wormed its way into Tara's chest, but she fought back with her justification. "He'd told me never to contact him again."

"I know. But he was angry. He didn't mean it. And then after it was said he didn't know how to take it back."

Kylee squealed and Tara's gaze followed the noise. Amanda had a piece of seaweed, and Kylee was running from it like it was a sea monster. Tara leaned back and turned to Rick again. "If my father really was sorry, why hadn't he tried to contact me before now?"

"I don't know. Maybe he was still angry you chose to marry Bobby against his advice."

"It wasn't his choice to make." She dug her fingers into the sand. The sun had warmed the top layer, but underneath it was cooler.

"I know. But what's done is done. He's reaching out to you and Kylee. Wouldn't it be a good thing to see if you can repair your relationship?"

She wanted to say something about Rick and his own relationship issues, but Tara stuffed the words down her throat. She didn't want to get into another fight with him. She gazed out over the ocean and forced herself to calm down. It wasn't a good idea to overreact. That only lead to embarrassment.

Rick sighed. "I'm sorry. I stuck my nose where it shouldn't have been. If you don't want to go visit your parents, I'll call Phil back and tell him it's off."

"No," she said, touching his arm. "It's okay. Maybe we could go see them."

He slid his arm around her and pulled her to his chest. "I won't let him hurt you again," he whispered, then he pressed his lips to the top of her head.

She snuggled into him, ignoring the little voice telling her not to get so close to Rick Shade. "I know," she said, her voice barely audible. Rick would do everything in his power to protect her and Kylee.

He wrapped both arms around her and she could smell his scent. A tiny hint of cologne mixed with a smell that was unique to Rick. Her heart beat faster.

He pulled back from her. "You know, if we were really married, I'd kiss you right now." His voice sounded raspy.

She looked up at him. "We *are* really married. I saw the paperwork."

His gaze dropped to her lips. "Then I guess I have to."

"Probably wouldn't be right if you didn't."

He leaned closer, stopping only a breath away from her lips. "I hope those onions I ate earlier don't ruin the kiss."

"I'll let you know if your breath is hideous by making little choking noises as we kiss."

His lips twitched. "Thanks," he said before he closed the gap. His soft lips teased hers, and she closed her eyes. His hand reached around her neck, pulling her closer, his thumb caressing her cheek. The kiss deepened and she lost all thought about what he'd eaten for lunch. Her skin tingled with his touch. She could easily melt into the sand and die a happy person.

"What are you doing, Mommy?" Kylee came bounding up to them, spraying sand on Tara's legs. She reluctantly pulled back.

"Kylee! Come here!" Amanda ran up to Kylee and picked her up. "I'm sorry, she got away from me."

Tara felt a blush creep up to her cheeks. "It's fine."

"Look at this!" Kylee said, holding up a seashell. Part of it had broken, revealing the intricate spiral on the inside.

Rick examined it. "That's awesome."

"Great find," Tara said, putting her hand up to shield her eyes from the sun.

"Let's go look for more treasures," Amanda said, holding out her hand. Kylee ran to her.

Rick turned toward Tara. "Where were we?"

Unfortunately, reality had set in and the moment was gone. She shouldn't be kissing Rick, not when their relationship had an expiration date. She needed to remember that even though the marriage certificate was real, what they had was fake.

"I was just about to tell you to keep it light on the onions next time."

His smile vanished. "Seriously?" He cupped his hand in front of his mouth and huffed into it, then sniffed.

Guilt made her stomach clench. The look on his face made it worse. He grimaced, like he'd just had one of his most embarrassing moments. She couldn't let him continue to think he had onion breath.

217

She laughed, trying to keep it light. "I'm just kidding."

His mouth dropped open and he poked her in the side. "I'm going to get you good for that one."

Before she knew it, he was on top of her, his knees straddling her sides, his fingers tickling under her ribs. She fell back against the sand and laughed, squirming to get away, but she couldn't. His fingers skimmed over her skin, making her laugh so hard she could barely breathe.

"Tickle me next!" Kylee said.

Rick finally relented, climbing off her and going after Kylee. Her daughter screamed and laughed as he chased her in the sand. Anyone watching would have thought he was her father. The thought made her blink back tears.

This, too, would end.

***

Rick wasn't sure why Tara's mood had shifted. After he fired up the grill and put the steaks on, he noticed she was acting aloof. He gripped the tongs in his hand and watched her and Kylee.

Maybe Tara was nervous to see her father again. Why had he intervened like that? If things went south when they visited, it would be his fault. He should have told her about the call and left things up to her.

But something inside of him had stirred when Phil said Tara's father just wanted to see his granddaughter. He wondered what he would have done if Scarlett had had his child and not told him. What lengths would he have gone to in order to see his daughter? Kylee was the epitome of cuteness. Rick loved the little squirt. Didn't Tara's father have the right to love her as well? They were family, after all.

He flipped one of the steaks and the meat sizzled. Kylee had all her shells and treasures she'd found at the beach spread out on the table. Tara smiled as Kylee showed her each one and chatted about it. He smiled despite his sour mood.

After dinner, he slipped outside and walked down to the water's edge. He watched as the waves came in, crashing against the rocks and sand. He'd messed things up yet again with Tara. Why couldn't he stay out of trouble with her? It seemed like no matter what happened, he always stuck his foot in it.

The sun crept lower in the sky, sending streaks of pink and gold across the clouds. He watched the birds flutter from the trees and soar above the waves. The sound of the water relaxed him. He sat on a rock and folded his hands in his lap.

He'd smooth things over with her . . . apologize or something. He needed her to be there for him. He was enjoying their conversations. They had a connection he'd never had with anyone before.

He was falling in love with her.

The thought shocked him, but as he let the notion sink in, he knew it was true. She saw him like no one else. Saw through him somehow. He hadn't even been aware of his deepening feelings, but now he couldn't deny them. Tara affected him like nothing else.

He swallowed the lump forming in his throat. One year. That was all he had with her. Then she would leave him. He wasn't sure he could bear it.

"Hey."

He turned around to find Tara standing a few feet away. She'd put on a jacket, as the temperature had dropped, and her hands were hidden in the pockets. He motioned for her to come sit by him on the rock.

"You all right?" she asked as she picked her way across the rocks.

"Yeah." He resumed his watch of the ocean.

"Kylee was so tired, I put her to bed early."

He nodded. "She sure liked telling you about those shells."

She chuckled and brushed a strand of hair from her face. "I can't believe she named them all."

Rick laughed, then they grew quiet. Only the sound of the waves and the birds pierced the silence. He could feel the crackle in the air between them. It was like the space itself was trying to pull them together.

Did she have to leave after the year?

He mentally shook his head. Why would she want to stay? He was a self-centered jerk who put his own career above everything else. No one in his life really wanted to be around him. Phil stuck by him because he paid him to. Everyone did. Heck, he'd even bought and paid for Tara.

What a fool.

Tara put her hand on his back. "This is beautiful. Thank you for sharing this with me. You don't mind that I came out here, do you?"

"No." He didn't mind at all. He'd rather spend as much time with her as he could, while she was still around.

Then another thought occurred to him. Maybe he could entice her to stay after the year was up. He could be charming. People often said he was handsome. He and Tara had chemistry. And for some reason, she kept forgiving him when he acted like a jerk. Maybe he could fan the flames. Make Tara fall in love with him.

He slid his arm around her and she laid her head on his shoulder. "It is a beautiful sight." He skimmed his hand over the skin on her arm. "And the sunset is pretty, too."

"Wow. Did you get that line from a gum wrapper?"

Ouch. And he thought he was being smooth. "Too corny?"

She laughed. "A bit much, yes."

He reached up and brushed his fingers across her cheek. The sunset cast an orange glow on her skin. "Sorry. I guess I just got caught up in the moment."

She closed her eyes, the breeze blowing the strands of hair that had come out of her ponytail.

"You still mad at me for agreeing to go see your father?"

She peeked at him with one eye open. "No."

"Good. Because I've been wanting to finish what we started." He hooked a finger under her chin and raised it, staring at her lips. "If it's okay with you," he added, not wanting to force her.

"I don't think that's a good idea," she said, turning her face away from him.

Rick clenched his jaw as the sting of rejection coursed through him. Trying to get Tara to fall in love with him was going to be harder than he thought. Maybe it wasn't a good idea after all.

He wasn't sure he could take any more rejection.

Chapter 20

ara swallowed the lump in her throat threatening to close off her breathing. Familiar streets flew by the passenger seat window. They were on their way to her parents' house. Why had she agreed to see her father again? She gripped the leather seat, her fingers turning white.

Rick squeezed her knee. "It'll be okay."

She glanced back at Kylee, asleep in her booster seat, hugging her Winnie the Pooh. Her hometown was two hours from the airport. Even though it was only four o'clock in the afternoon, the long drive had done her in.

"I hope this was the right decision."

"Tell me about growing up. Did you have a good relationship with your father before the fall-out?"

How could she best describe it? "It was more like living with a dictator than a father." That was harsh. Her father had been strict and emotionally pulled back, but that might be taking it a bit too far.

Rick cringed. "That bad?"

"He was always right. You didn't go against his wishes. I found that out the hard way when I married Bobby. And now I'm married again. And no offense, but he won't be happy about our marriage, since you're always in the papers."

"What does he do for a living?"

"He's a cop."

Rick tugged on his collar. "Really?" Beads of sweat broke out on his brow.

"Don't worry. It will be okay." She couldn't help but smile as she said it.

He chuckled, but Tara saw him swallow hard as he pulled in front of her childhood home. "We're here. Quick, get the kid. We can use her as a shield."

Tara whacked him on the arm, but smiled nonetheless. She carefully unbuckled Kylee, gathering her into her arms. Kylee rubbed her eyes and yawned. "Where are we?"

"We're at Grandma and Grandpa's house."

Kylee placed her head on Tara's shoulder and buried her face into her neck. Rick put his hand on the small of Tara's back as they walked to the door. The door swung open and Tara's mother, Joyce, stepped out onto the stoop. "Tara," she said, enveloping her in her arms. "I'm so happy to see you."

Seeing her mother again was like a balm to her soul. She blinked back tears. "How are you, Mom?"

"I'm good." She pulled back and smiled at Kylee. "My granddaughter?"

Tara nodded. "Kylee."

Joyce gave Kylee a kiss on the cheek. "Please, come in."

The smell of something cooking met her as she walked in. The living room seemed dark compared to the outdoors, and Tara's vision took a second to adjust. Her father stood by his favorite recliner, his face a stony mask. His hair had thinned a bit, and now had grey streaks. His firm jaw and broad chest hadn't changed.

Tara cleared her throat. "Mom, Dad, this is Rick," she said, introducing him. "And this is Kylee." The little girl looked around the room at the various gnome statues Joyce had collected over the years.

Tara motioned to her parents. "This is Joyce and Douglas McDermott."

Rick stuck out his hand to her father. "Nice to meet you, sir." When he turned to Joyce, she held out her arms for a hug, which Rick awkwardly accepted.

"Please sit down," her mother said.

Tara and Rick sat on the couch. Tara smoothed her fingers over the orange flowered upholstery she'd lain on when she had tonsillitis as a child. Her childhood home had not changed much, if at all.

Douglas sat in his recliner and Joyce pulled a chair in from the dining room. "How old is she?" her mother asked after seating herself.

"She just turned four."

Douglas finally spoke. "I can't believe you didn't tell us about our own grandchild."

Her mother shot him a warning glare. "Doug, please."

He closed his eyes and pinched the bridge of his nose. "I'm sorry. My wife seems to think we need to mend fences."

So he wasn't the one who wanted to patch things up after all. She should have figured that out. Joyce quickly stood. "Does anyone want anything to drink? We have soda or water or iced tea."

Rick glanced at Tara before answering. "I'll take a glass of water."

"Water is fine, Mom," Tara said.

Kylee buried her face into Tara's shirt. Her mother rushed from the room and came back a moment later with two glasses of ice water. She set them on the coffee table in front of them. "How was your flight?"

"It was fine," Rick said.

Tension hung in the room like a thick cloud, making it hard to breathe. Tara rubbed Kylee's back. "Do you want to say hi to your grandma?"

Kylee shook her head and covered her face with her hands. Great. The clock ticked the seconds as everyone sat. Her head spun as she tried to think of something she could do. Anything to dispel the awkwardness. Nothing came to mind.

Her mother stood. "I almost forgot. I have something for Kylee." She rushed into the other room and came back with a gift bag decorated with blue and yellow elephants. She held it out.

"That's for you," Tara said, nudging Kylee to take it. Her daughter still wasn't fully awake, but she took the gift from Joyce and peered into the bag.

Kylee pulled out a set of plastic keys. "That's a baby toy," she said, a frown on her face.

Tara felt like crawling under the carpet. "Say, 'thank you,' Kylee."

"Thank you," Kylee said, tossing the keys on the couch.

Joyce twisted her fingers together. "I wasn't sure what to get." She motioned to the bag. "There's something else in there."

Kylee stuck her hand back in the bag and rustled the paper. She pulled out a stuffed elephant and hugged it to her chest. "Thank you," she said.

Joyce smiled at the reaction. "You're welcome."

The awkward silence settled in again until Rick shifted and looked at her father. "Tara tells me you're a police officer. How long have you been on the force?"

"I'm retired now," her father said. "A fact she would know if she hadn't gone off and married that idiot actor."

Joyce sat up straight and glared. "Can't we put that behind us?"

"I can't see how. She's gone and done it again."

Rick stiffened. He put his hand on Tara's shoulder protectively. "Maybe we should be going."

Joyce stood. "No. Please, stay. There's a roast in the oven. I'd really like for you to eat dinner with us."

Her father got up from his chair and crossed the room. "I don't need to be disrespected like this in my own home." He grabbed his keys and opened the front door. "I meant what I said. I don't have a daughter anymore." He left, slamming the door behind him.

Tara's throat constricted and she tried to blink back the tears. This was worse than she'd expected. And she hadn't expected a lot. Rick pulled her close in a one-arm embrace.

Joyce exhaled and rubbed her temples. Tara handed Kylee to Rick and walked to her mother, taking her into her arms. "I'm so sorry. I didn't mean to cause any more damage. We'll leave."

"Your father is just upset. He'll come around." Joyce pulled back, a pained look on her face. "It will all be fine. You'll see. Please stay for dinner."

Tara glanced at Rick to gauge his reaction. "It's up to you," he said.

"Alright, we'll stay, but if he comes back it will probably be best if we go."

Her mother nodded, and Tara realized how much older she looked. Maybe the stress had aged her. Joyce took a step back. "That's fine."

"Do you need any help in the kitchen?" Tara asked.

Her mother ushered her back to the couch. "No, not for another hour. Let's just sit and talk."

Rick shifted Kylee on his lap. "I can't help but notice all your gnomes. Tell me about them."

Her mother blushed. "I've been collecting gnomes for as long as I can remember. Most I found at garage sales or thrift stores." She crossed the room and picked up one from a shelf. "A few of them are Tom Clark gnomes, and those are worth a little money, but the rest are just fun to have."

She handed Rick the figure. "This one is signed by Tom."

Rick turned the sculpture over in his hand. The gnome sat on a stump and held a teddy bear. "Nice," he said, handing it back. Tara figured he was just being polite. Her mother's gnome obsession was a bit weird.

Her mother put the gnome back and sat down. "Tell me, how did you guys meet?"

Kylee snuggled into Rick's chest, still clutching her toy elephant. Rick gave Tara a loaded look before speaking. "Tara was my housekeeper. When I saw her, I was instantly attracted to her. I don't know . . . something about her eyes." He winked at her, and her heart stuttered. "We started dating, and things took off rather quickly from there." Rick's fingers grazed her arm, and tingles erupted. Why did his touch always do that to her? "She's pretty amazing."

Tara had to remind herself that Rick was an actor. This is what he was good at. And man was he good at it. She wanted to dump her glass of ice water on herself. "Thanks," she said, forcing a demure smile. Then she turned to her mother. "I fell in love with Rick as I got to know the man he is deep inside. He's the kind of man who would dole out a compliment to a kid, just to give them a nice memory. He's tender-hearted. He wouldn't do anything to hurt anyone else." As she spoke, she tried to keep her voice steady, for while Rick was acting, she realized her own words were true.

She loved Rick.

The thought made her draw in a quick breath, which unfortunately came with a wad of spit and she immediately started coughing. Was she really in love with Rick? Her mother wrung her hands as Tara struggled to breathe.

Rick patted her on the back. "You okay?"

She coughed some more, unable to speak. Nodding, she picked up her water and took a gulp. When she could breathe, she managed to say, "I'm fine. Just breathed in funny."

A look she couldn't interpret crossed Rick's face before he smiled. "Well, that was exciting."

Joyce clutched at her imitation pearl necklace. "Do you need more water?"

"No, Mom, I'm fine." Tara took another breath to show everyone she knew how to breathe properly.

"I made a cheesecake for dessert."

Rick grinned. "Now you're talking."

Tara let them talk about the food while she revisited the idea that she was in love with Rick Shade. His touch sent her heart into overdrive, that was for sure. And his smile . . . he didn't just have one. She'd learned to discern his many different smiles. He had one he put on for the cameras. One for when he was uncomfortable. But then there were the ones he let her see when no one else was around. The smile that crinkled his eyes. That was the one he used when they were playing around.

Just thinking about his smile made her feel all giddy. He had a hard exterior, but she knew it was because he'd been hurt in the past. Inside, he truly cared about people. She stared out the window at her parents' front lawn. Yes, she loved him. That was the only explanation for the way she felt.

And she had no idea what she was going to do about it.

Chapter 21

Rick stabbed a piece of beef and put it in his mouth. The thing almost melted. He held back a moan. He'd never tasted anything so good. "This is delicious."

Joyce smiled, her cheeks turning pink. "Thank you."

Kylee sat beside Tara with a dictionary under her because Joyce had worried she couldn't reach. Kylee gleefully spooned mashed potatoes in her mouth.

"Mom loves to cook," Tara said, taking a bite. "For some reason, I didn't get her talent."

"I think in order to learn to cook, one has to spend time in the kitchen." Joyce gave her daughter a playful smile.

"Sorry, I never got too interested in it."

"She was more interested in studying. She graduated with a 4.0 GPA, did she tell you that? She was valedictorian of her class." Joyce straightened her back.

Tara's face flushed. "No one cares about high school, Mom."

"That's an impressive accomplishment," Rick said. He was beginning to realize what a sacrifice it was for Tara to work while Bobby went to college.

Tara shrugged away his admiration. "Doesn't mean anything now. I'm just a maid."

Joyce dropped her fork and it made a clanging noise. "You're not just a maid. You're the wife of a movie star. Surely you can do anything you want to do."

Tara's eyes widened. "Oh, yes, well. I meant I was just a maid before." She coughed and slouched down in her seat.

Kylee giggled and dropped her fork on her own plate, so it made another loud noise. Tara touched her daughter's hand. "Grandma dropped her fork on accident, honey. Don't do it on purpose."

Rick took a sip of his water and wondered if Tara wanted to enroll in some classes. He filed it away to bring up later. "Joyce, tell me a little more about yourself. What is it you do?"

"I work down at the county clerk's office. Just pushing papers and answering phones."

Tara raised her eyebrows like she hadn't known this. "How long have you worked there?"

"About two years."

The front door opened and Douglas walked in. He deposited his keys in a bowl and walked into the kitchen. No one moved. Only the sound of the living room clock ticking permeated the room. A moment later he came into the dining room with a fork and plate and sat down. He proceeded to fill his plate, not saying a word.

Kylee wiggled in her chair. Tara leaned over. "Do you need to go to the bathroom?"

Kylee nodded, and Tara took her daughter into the other room. Douglas continued to eat. Joyce sat quietly, watching her husband. The term awkward didn't come close to the situation.

Rick decided the silence was too much for him to take. "You two have a lovely home."

Joyce smiled at him. "Thank you, Rick."

"What made you settle here in Iowa?"

Douglas picked up a napkin and wiped his mouth. "We both grew up here. No reason to leave."

"How did you meet?" Rick figured if he kept asking questions, at some point the awkwardness would evaporate.

"We met in high school. On a blind date," Douglas said.

"Actually, you only thought it was a blind date."

"What?" Douglas stared at his wife.

"I wanted to go out with you, but I was afraid you'd say no, so I schemed a little." She picked up her water glass and took a sip, a smug look on her face.

"And I'm just now finding out about this?"

"Had no reason to tell you after we hit it off."

Tara walked back into the room with Kylee, and Douglas burst out laughing. Tara raised an eyebrow. "What's so funny?"

"Apparently your mother has hidden the real story of how we met for the last twenty years."

Tara lifted Kylee onto her seat. "What do you mean? You didn't meet on a blind date?"

Everyone looked at Joyce. She fidgeted in her chair. "I asked my best friend Patty to help me get a date with this cute guy at school. Patty was a cashier down at the hardware store where his uncle worked, so she talked to Mike and set things up."

"All this time I thought Uncle Mike knew you from his youth program."

Joyce looked at her husband through lowered lids. "Mike coached junior league football. He made up the story about the youth program."

Douglas roared with laughter again.

Kylee giggled, at first a little nervously, but her giggles made everyone else laugh.

"What's funny, Kylee?" Tara asked.

"I don't know," she said while giggling. Everyone cracked up.

The tension dissipated after that. When they were done eating, Rick offered to help with the dishes, but Joyce and Tara shooed him into the living room with Douglas. He wondered if they needed time alone to chat.

Rick sat down on the couch as Tara's father reclined in his chair. Unfortunately, the awkwardness came back in full force. Douglas picked up a newspaper and Rick fingered the Good Housekeeping magazines stacked in the bottom of the coffee table. With nothing else to do, he picked one up and began leafing through it.

After ten minutes of looking at recipes and furniture, Rick tossed the magazine back and rubbed his hands together. "So, do you miss being on the force?"

Tara's father lowered his newspaper and stared him down. "I'd rather talk about my daughter. What are you doing with her?"

Rick choked and pounded his fist on his chest. "Excuse me?"

"I've read the articles. I know what kind of man you are. Why are you married to my daughter?"

Rick glanced outside. They get tornadoes in Iowa, right? Why couldn't one come ripping through town right about now? He tugged on his collar. "Don't believe what you read in the papers."

A scowl crossed Douglas's face. "Were you drunk when you proposed?"

Dinner sat in Rick's stomach like a rock. "We were at a club. I had a few—"

"And were you drunk when you dragged her to a Las Vegas chapel?"

Rick held up his hand. "No. I hadn't been drinking the night we got married. We—"

"Do you love her?"

The question hit him in the gut. He did love her. He just didn't think she loved him back. He cleared his throat and spoke from his heart. "Yes. I love your daughter, and I adore your granddaughter. I would never do anything to hurt

242

either one of them. Your daughter is smart . . . and funny. She sometimes takes life too seriously, but I love that about her, too. I love the way her hair falls down her back when she lets me pull it out of that blasted bun. I love her smile, the way her lips curl up, and the way it lights up her eyes."

Douglas studied him for a moment. "Good. Because if you treat her like that other punk did . . ." His voice cracked but his threat never materialized.

Rick shook his head. "Of course not," he said. "I'd never . . ."

Tara cleared her throat and Rick turned to see her standing in the archway between the living room and the dining room, her arms folded. He wasn't sure how much of the conversation she had heard. "Dishes are done. Does anyone want cheesecake?"

"Yes, thank you," Rick said, glancing over at her father. Douglas nodded.

They ate dessert, the conversation staying away from important things.

***

Tara laid her sleeping daughter on the guest bed and pulled the covers up, tucking her in. She turned the nightlight on and closed the door. If Kylee woke up in the night, she'd be on the other side of the wall and would hear her cries.

Tara stood in the hallway, her hand on her heart. She'd heard what Rick had said to her father. No wonder they paid him the big bucks. He was an amazing actor. She almost believed him when he professed his love.

And her father? Had he really gotten that upset about Bobby? It was the first time she'd seen any sign of him getting emotional over her. She knew he'd been mad when she married Bobby, but she thought it was because she was going against his wishes. This was the first time she realized it might be something else.

She slipped into the room that was her childhood bedroom. Everything was the same, down to the photos of her friends she had tacked to the corkboard around her mirror. They'd even left her old TV on her dresser. Rick sat on the bed in his usual lounge pants and t-shirt. "Did she sleep through you putting on her pajamas?"

"Yes. We wore her out with all the running in the backyard."

"I must admit, I was a little jealous. I wanted to swing on that tire."

Tara laughed. "I might pay good money to see that."

He sobered. "Can I ask you something?"

Tara picked up her nightgown and leaned against the doorjamb of the tiny adjoining bathroom. "Yes."

"Do you want to go back to school?"

Tara had not expected that at all. She thought about how to best choose her words. "I have to focus on Kylee right now."

"Amanda can watch Kylee. If money were no object, would you enroll in college?"

Tara picked at her fingernail. She'd love nothing more than to go to college, but unfortunately, money *was* an object. It wasn't realistic, even with the hundred thousand he was going to pay her. She had so much debt stacked up from Bobby taking her to court, most of it would go to paying that off. And what little would be left would be eaten up in a down payment on a small place to live. "I think my time has passed."

Rick stood and crossed the room, leaning one hand against the wall. His close proximity made her heart jump. He smelled good. "Of course not. You're young and smart. You're not past anything. What were you planning on majoring in before you married Bobby?"

Tara broke his gaze. "I wanted to study French literature."

A slow smile spread across his face. "You're ambitious. One thing I like about you."

"Just one?" Why did she say that? She needed to stop flirting.

His grin widened. "There's many more."

She knew he'd flirt back. They'd been playing this game ever since they ran off to Las Vegas two weeks ago. She had to stop, though. It was hard on her heart. She took a step back. "Well, school was just a dream. I have to raise a daughter, and the money you're paying me is all going to settle my debt and get us a new start. There won't be any left for college."

His smile vanished, and his jaw worked. He looked like he wanted to say something else, but simply nodded and backed up.

She hugged her nightgown to her chest. "I'm going to change and get ready for bed."

"Okay."

After she was done in the bathroom she made her way through the dim light to the bed. Rick was on the far side, already under the covers. They'd been sharing a bed since the wedding, and Rick hadn't made any moves on her, but this was not a king-sized bed. She'd have to sleep right next to him. She swallowed and climbed in.

"I can sleep on the floor if you're uncomfortable."

"I'm fine," she said, her voice squeaking. Smooth.

Rick chuckled. "I'll sleep with my back to you. Would that help?"

"Thanks." She turned over as well, their backs now pressed against each other. The warmth from the contact seeped through her nightgown. She sighed. Sleep might take a while to come to her tonight.

"If you wanted to take a few classes . . . while we're still married, I mean . . . I think it would be a great idea," he said, his voice quiet in the darkness.

She bit her lip. Would she even dare to start something like that, just to have to stop when they divorced? She'd hate to start something she couldn't finish, but it would be stupid of her not to take him up on his offer. "I'll think about it."

"Don't think for too long. Fall registration is happening now, I'm sure."

She smiled even though he couldn't see her. Start college? Her excitement grew at the thought. She could really start classes in a few months, if she wanted to? That was almost too good to be true. She clutched the covers. "Thanks, Rick."

He didn't answer.

Chapter 22

ick sat back in the lounge chair, a cold Diet Coke in his hand. The bright sun made it hard to see without squinting. He slid on his sunglasses. Kylee squealed and giggled as Tara pushed her on the tire swing. Douglas and Joyce sat with Rick on the patio, watching their granddaughter.

Joyce turned to Rick. "What movie are you working on?"

He forced a smile. "I'm between movies right now, but there are some things coming down the pike that look promising." He'd said the words so many times, he could say them without thought.

"Ooh, really? Can you talk about them?" Joyce's eyes lit up.

"No, not really." Easy way out of that.

Her gaze fell. "Oh."

Dang. Now she was disappointed. He leaned forward. "But if you can keep a secret, I did audition for a new Disney film. I'm not allowed to say which one, but the script is epic."

She grinned conspiratorially. "I won't tell a soul. How exciting!"

Kylee wiggled down from the tire swing and ran to Douglas. "Come play with me!" She tugged on his hand.

He hesitated, but then a smile spread across his face. "Alright." He crossed the grass with her and lifted her gently onto the tire swing, almost like she was made of glass.

Tara came and sat down on Douglas's chair. She wiped her forehead. "Man, she wears me out."

"Just like you when you were that age," Joyce said.

Tara smiled. Rick loved the way it reached her eyes. "I did love to run, didn't I?"

Douglas laughed at something Kylee said.

"I know he's still angry I married Bobby. But he seems to be mellowing out a little since yesterday's outburst," Tara said.

"He just wants what's best for you. You know that, don't you?" Joyce said.

Tara nodded. "Yes, I think I understand it better now. When he kicked me out, I thought he was mad at me. Hated me, even. Now I see he was trying to protect me from myself. He was trying to keep me from getting hurt, but he didn't know how to do it."

Joyce worried her hands together. "We saw how immature Bobby was. How self-centered he could be. He loved you in the way a person loves a hamburger. He wanted to use you to satisfy his hunger. But a marriage needs to be built on more. You need the kind of love that puts the other person first."

Rick blinked. He'd never thought about it that way before, but it made perfect sense. Was he putting Tara first, or wanting to use her? Obviously, he hadn't started out loving her at all. The whole situation was for their mutual benefit. But now that he had feelings for her, he wasn't sure where he stood.

Her long-term goal was to move back to the Midwest. He could see the draw. Clear skies, green grass, and the air smelled fresh and clean. Would he be acting selfish if he proposed she stay with him in L.A.?

He had a sinking feeling in his stomach that he was treating Tara like a hamburger.

Douglas came back over to the group of adults. A scraping noise rang out as he pulled another folding chair over to them. Kylee was now picking dandelions.

"How long are you planning on staying?" Douglas asked.

"I thought we'd leave tomorrow, if it's okay to stay another night," Rick said.

"That's fine."

"We're glad you came." Joyce lowered her gaze. "We weren't sure you would."

Rick reached out and took Tara's hand. He wasn't sure why, but he thought maybe she needed the reassurance. Tara looked like she was working up the courage to say something. Finally, she said, "I'm sorry for running off with Bobby." She lifted her gaze to meet her father's. "You were right about him."

Her father set his jaw. His fingers tapped on the sides of his chair. "I shouldn't have kicked you out." He didn't look like he was done, so no one said anything. Time seemed to tick by slowly as everyone waited for him to finish. "I was wrong."

No one moved for a few heartbeats. Then Tara blinked a few times. "It's all in the past."

A tension hung in the air for a moment before Joyce said, "Where's Kylee?"

Rick quickly scanned the backyard but didn't see her. Tara jumped out of her chair. "Kylee!" she called.

The backyard wasn't fenced in, but hedges surrounded the area. It would be most likely that she wandered on into the front yard. Rick walked around the side of the house, checking the bushes and behind the air conditioning unit to see if she were hiding. "Kylee?"

With no sign of the little girl, his concern grew, especially when he saw Tara, Douglas, and Joyce coming around the other side of the house without her.

"Kylee!" Tara yelled, her face pale, her gaze scanning the street.

"Mommy!"

Bobby stepped out from behind the neighbor's tree, carrying Kylee on one hip. Kylee grinned, one arm hugging Bobby's neck. "Daddy's here."

Acid boiled up in Rick's stomach and he marched over to Bobby. Tara ran and took Kylee. She wrapped Kylee in her arms protectively and backed away from her ex.

Anger pulsed through Rick. He swung a fist and punched Bobby in the right eye. Bobby went down like someone cut his puppet strings. Rick wasn't expecting that at all, and just stared at him sprawled out on the ground. Joyce sucked in a breath and Tara said, "Oh!"

Bobby clutched his eye and moaned. Then he stood and pointed to Rick, his pain suddenly gone. He looked at something across the street. "Did you get that?"

A man stepped out from the shadows holding a camera with a zoom lens. "Yep."

Rick's anger intensified, filling his chest with heat. "You did this on purpose? To set me up?"

"I'm calling the police," Douglas said.

Bobby grinned. "Yes! Call the police. I want to press charges."

"I'm calling because you tried to kidnap my granddaughter," Douglas said, almost growling.

Bobby held up his hands. "Whoa, I didn't take Kylee. She came running to me when she saw me. I'm on a public sidewalk." He took a step off the grass so his statement could be true. "I'm her father and I have a right to see her."

What a lowlife. It made Rick sick to see Bobby using Kylee like that. He wanted to pound him into the ground. Rick grabbed Bobby's shirt in his fists. A satisfied grin spread across Bobby's face. "Go ahead. He's still filming."

Rick released Bobby and took several steps back. He dragged his hand through his hair, trying to calm his anger. Nothing good would come from him beating up Bobby on camera. Shoot, he was already in trouble. People would flock to Bobby's defense, given the footage the man across the street had. Rick realized his career could be completely over if that surfaced.

No one seemed to know what to do. Douglas stood frozen, his phone out but not making a move to call the police like he'd threatened. Joyce and Tara shielded Kylee from Bobby. Rick stared at the smug look on Bobby's face. He'd won.

"I'd hate for that video to get out," Bobby said, smoothing his shirt.

"I bet you would," Rick said under his breath. How had Tara ever seen anything good in this guy? He was slimy. And from the look on Tara's face, she was thinking the exact same thing.

"I think we can all come to an understanding." Bobby stuck his hands in his pockets and looked up at the sky like he was commenting on the good weather.

The only understanding Rick wanted was the one where his fist was down Bobby's throat. He shouldn't have given in to Bobby in the first place. This had gotten out of control. And now there was no way to stuff the genie back in the bottle. He'd probably spend the rest of his life doing whatever Bobby wanted in order to keep Tara and Kylee safe.

A small movement from Douglas caught his eye. He had opened his camera app, the lens still pointed to the ground. Rick returned his gaze to Bobby, praying Douglas would turn on his video recorder. "What do you want, Bobby?"

"I want your agent to get me some auditions."

Perfect. Rick resisted the temptation to glance at Douglas's phone. "Just auditions?"

Bobby froze, a look of glee spreading across his face. "Can you rig the auditions?"

What a slimeball. And an idiot on top of it. "Is that what you want?"

A hungry look came into Bobby's eyes. "Yes. I want a part. Not just anything. A good one."

"And if I can't get you that?" Rick asked.

Bobby glanced back at the guy across the street. "The video will come out."

Rick nodded, pretending to think about it. "What about Kylee?"

"If you get me a big enough part, I'll be too busy to use my allotted time with her. You'll be rid of me."

"Hmm." Rick frowned. "I can't believe I fell for your setup. Pretty clever, staging something like this."

Bobby chuckled. "I'm not as stupid as people think."

Rick turned to Douglas. "You getting all this?"

"Oh, yeah," Douglas said, turning the phone up so it was now recording Bobby's face.

Rick turned back to Bobby, who had lost his smug look. "I have you on tape blackmailing me. You basically just admitted you set me up."

Bobby's face turned white. "Hey, now, I didn't—"

"Listen." Rick took a step toward Bobby, who backed up and bumped against the tree. Rick stuck his finger in Bobby's face. "I'm going to sue you for everything you're worth. You might be able to put up a decent fight in court, but I have more resources than you do, and better lawyers. I can drag this thing on until you have nothing left."

Sweat broke out on Bobby's forehead. Rick continued. "You are a sorry excuse for a human being. You treat your daughter as a pawn. I'm going to take this tape to court and sever your parental rights."

"You can't do that," Bobby said, his voice squeaking.

"Maybe not, but you'll spend months in court fighting it. Is that really how you want to spend your money?"

Bobby swallowed, his Adam's apple rising and falling. He took a step to the side around the tree and backed away from Rick. "Look, I didn't mean to cause any trouble."

Tara took a step toward Bobby, still cradling Kylee to her chest. "You didn't mean any trouble? How long have you been waiting outside my parents' house? I wonder if the neighbors have seen you hanging around. I bet the police would be really interested in what you're doing lurking around the neighborhood."

Bobby retreated further. "I'm not—this isn't what it looks like. I think this has been a big misunderstanding." He held his palms out. "I think we're all fine here. No need to do anything rash."

"I'm glad we've gotten everything sorted out," Rick said.

Bobby gave them a pathetic smile. "So we're good?"

Tara hugged Kylee close. "Leave, Bobby."

Bobby turned and jogged toward his car. Rick exhaled, not realizing he had been holding his breath.

Chapter 23

ara couldn't stop shaking. She sat in her parents' living room, holding Kylee on her lap. As soon as Kylee realized her father was leaving, she'd wailed. Rick had taken her and consoled her until she stopped crying, but Tara needed to hold her daughter. She couldn't believe she'd let Kylee slip away from her. Those brief moments when she didn't know where Kylee was had terrified her.

Rick sat down next to Tara and handed her a glass of ice water. "Here, drink this."

She took a gulp, the icy water sliding down her throat, numbing her.

"He's gone. He won't come back." Rick wrapped his arm around her, his contact sending her heart into overdrive.

"How can you be sure?"

"He just wanted leverage so I would do his bidding. He doesn't have that anymore. We have evidence. He's not going to want to risk that getting out."

"What about . . . ?" She looked down at Kylee, who had snuggled in and closed her eyes.

"We can't legally stop him from seeing her. But when they have visits, I can hire protection for her, so we make sure he won't ever take her and run."

Tara couldn't believe he would do that for her. "Really?"

He rubbed her back. "Of course. I just want Kylee to be safe."

That's all she wanted as well, but after a year, they'd no longer be anything to each other. Maybe he could protect Kylee now, but that would eventually end. And then she'd be on her own, wondering if Bobby was going to go off the deep end again. But her parents were sitting in the room with them, so she wasn't able to say anything. "Thanks."

At the end of the day, Tara was exhausted. She put Kylee to bed, went into the other room and slipped under the covers, ready to put the day behind her. Rick rolled over. "Are you all right? You were quiet at dinner."

"Just tired."

His fingers brushed her cheek. "I'll protect her."

Tara's pulse raced. She knew he meant it. The sincerity was in his eyes. He cared about Kylee. And Kylee adored him, that was certain. She clung to him every chance she got. He was so gentle with her. Kylee couldn't help but fall in love with him.

His eyebrows pulled together in concern. His thumb grazed her cheek. "You're crying."

Was she? She blinked and wiped at her cheeks. Stupid. She didn't need to be thinking about how he had won Kylee over. How her daughter adored another man who was going to leave them. How Tara would feel after Rick was gone.

Pain stabbed in her chest. Rick would be the perfect father for Kylee. "Would" being the important word. It wasn't real. He was acting. This was just another gig for him. She broke his gaze. "Sorry."

"Don't apologize. What Bobby did scared me to death. I totally get why you're emotional about it." He gathered her into his arms.

Warmth enveloped her and she laid her cheek on his muscular arm, snuggling into him. It might only be temporary, but she had one year with him. She could enjoy it while it lasted.

She closed her eyes and fell asleep, wrapped in his arms.

***

Rick awoke to the sound of "The Imperial March." He tried to untangle himself from Tara without waking her, but she raised her head and blinked her eyes. "Phil's calling? That can't be good."

"It never is," he said, suddenly grumpy Phil had awoken them. He was enjoying the feeling of Tara in his arms. He picked up the phone and swiped to answer. "Yes?"

"Turn on the celebrity news."

"What? Why?"

"Just do it." Phil sounded impatient, so Rick slid out of bed and crossed the room. He flicked on the small TV sitting on Tara's dresser. He messed with the channels until he got what he wanted.

". . . serious allegation. Can you substantiate it with any facts?" A reporter stuck a microphone into a man's face. He had white-tipped hair and looked slightly familiar.

"I heard it from Rick Shade himself. He married her to settle down his party boy image."

Tara gasped, and Rick's chest tightened. Who was that guy?

"Liam," Tara said, answering his unspoken question. "The limo driver," she whispered, her hand raising to her mouth. "Oh, no."

Rick turned to her. "It's okay. It's his word against ours."

Liam pulled out his phone. "And I have this."

Rick's voice came out of the television. "It's okay, this doesn't mess up our plan. No one knows we're just doing this for publicity. We're still on track. Everything will be fine."

Rick's heart sank. Liam had proof. His phone began playing the Darth Vader song again and he wiped his sweaty hands on his t-shirt before picking it up. "Yes?"

"We can't come back from this." Phil sounded defeated. "It's in your own voice that this is just a publicity stunt. There's no use lying anymore."

Desperation grew in Rick. He didn't want to give up. He needed more time with Tara. "Forget them. Who cares what people think?"

"That's the whole reason we're doing this!" Phil let out an exasperated grunt. "Listen, I've got to come out with a statement. We'll come clean.

Make a joke out of it or something. Another crazy Rick Shade stunt."

Rick knew it was no use fighting it. Phil was right. This was the only way to save face. If he could even save his reputation. "Alright," he said, and hung up.

Tara worried her lip, her hands clasped together. He didn't want to have to tell her. He scratched his chin, trying to think of what to say. "We're coming clean. Phil's going to release a statement. Admit that this was all for publicity."

Her shoulders fell. "I see."

"We don't have to pretend anymore. You are officially released from your contract."

She looked like she was going to cry. He hadn't thought about it before, but she was counting on that money to give her a new start. He rushed on to say, "I'll still pay you. It's in the contract. You married me and upheld your end of the bargain. I'm the one ending it early."

She turned away from him. "Thanks," she said quietly.

"And if you need any help with Bobby, just call me. I don't want Kylee going to see him without someone else there. I don't trust that man."

Tara nodded, still facing away from him.

He couldn't stand to see her upset. "And I still think you should enroll in college. I'll pay for it."

She faced him, her cheeks white. "No, you don't have to. Not with everything else you're doing. I couldn't accept that."

He wanted to pull her into his arms and tell her he wanted to do it for her . . . because he loved her. But his feet stayed rooted to the carpet. If he told her, she'd think he was just being impulsive. Rash. Like he always was. Jumping into things without thinking.

He glanced around the room, unsure of what to look at. Things were starting to turn awkward. "Do you want to stay here then, since your plan was to move to Iowa? Or do you want to come back to L.A. with me?" Could he dare hope she'd want to return with him?

"My parents don't watch celebrity news. I'd rather leave with you, then find a way to break it to them later."

Thinking of Douglas and all his questioning the other night, Rick agreed. "That would be best." Rick didn't want to be anywhere near her father when he found out the whole marriage was a sham.

They began packing and getting ready for their trip. When Rick went downstairs, he found Kylee sitting at the table with Joyce and Douglas. A stack of waffles sat in the middle of the table. Kylee had a bowl of blueberries and was putting a berry in each dimple of her waffle.

"Good morning," he said.

Douglas stood and clapped him on the back. "Rick. You can have my chair. I was just finishing up."

The difference in Douglas was like night and day. He was relaxed. Smiling. Almost jovial. Joyce seemed happier, too. "Thanks," Rick said, sitting down.

Joyce took a clean plate from a stack and handed it to him. "Have as many as you'd like. They're still warm."

Kylee got done with her blueberries, then started eating them one at a time, counting as she went.

"You know your numbers," Joyce said. "Good job."

"And I know my alphy-bet too."

"You do? Show me."

Kylee rattled off letters, missing a few as she went. Joyce patted her on the head when she was done. "Very good."

Tara joined them. After breakfast, Rick helped clear the dishes. Joyce took the stack of plates from him. "You can go sit in the living room."

"Actually, you may have missed it, but I believe I made headline news the other day when I did such an awesome job drying the dishes."

Tara snorted and ducked her head.

Joyce tossed him a towel. "Well, that would be nice of you."

Tara filled the sink with soapy water and Kylee climbed up on a chair to "help." Rick glanced around the kitchen. "You've never had a dishwasher?"

Joyce motioned to Tara. "Had one for years before she moved out."

He chuckled. "Tara still insists on doing the dishes in the sink. Even with a state-of-the-art dishwasher at home."

"She's always liked hand-washing them." Joyce shrugged. "I don't mind it either. Gives me time to think."

Tara washed the plates and rinsed them off, handing them to Rick. He dried them and put them in the cupboard. Joyce watched the two of them. "I wasn't sure what to think about the two of you. But I can see, you two really do love each other."

Tara sucked in a breath and then had a coughing fit. Rick tried to cover for her after she left the room. "Yes, I do love your daughter. She's very special."

Joyce patted his cheeks. "You take care of her."

Guilt rose like a wave in his throat, making it hard to breathe. "Of course."

He set the towel down and started loading the rental car with their things. Kylee wanted to help, so he gave her their pillows and other light items to carry. When the car was ready, he picked Kylee up and headed back inside.

Tara was in the living room with her parents. She glanced at Rick. "All loaded?"

"Yep."

"I guess this is it." Tara hugged her mother, then awkwardly looked at her father.

Douglas pulled her into a hug. "Don't stay away too long."

Rick's gut twisted at this. Douglas didn't have to worry. Tara would be back soon. Kylee gave each of her grandparents a hug and kiss, with a little prompting from Tara. Then they were out the door. Rick buckled Kylee in her booster seat, then turned to Tara, who looked like she was starting to get emotional. "You'll see them soon."

His words didn't seem to help. "I know," she said under her breath. She turned away from him and got into the car.

Rick felt like a jerk for some reason, but wasn't sure why.

Chapter 24

ara stared at the clothes in her closet. No, Rick's closet. Rick's clothes. None of it was hers. She slowly closed the doors. She had nothing to pack, except for a few outfits she'd brought, and Kylee's things, which she shoved in the garbage bag she'd brought with her.

Trash. That's what she felt like. Rick was done with her, and now she was being thrown away. She swallowed and shook her head. She was being ridiculous. She agreed to this for the money, and now it was ending. She was getting what she wanted. A new life with Kylee.

So why did it feel so empty?

Kylee sat on the floor playing with her Jenga blocks, her favorite ladybug shirt on. She'd stack a few up, then use Winnie the Pooh to knock them down. Her giggles rang out. Tara crouched down beside her. "Time to pack these up. We need to head out."

Kylee looked up at her with her big, brown eyes. "Where are we going?"

"To a new adventure."

She looked up to see Rick standing in the doorway. Kylee noticed too and went running to him. She hugged his legs. "Rick's coming, too?"

Tara's eyes stung, and her chest tightened. "No."

Rick picked Kylee up and she threw her arms around his neck. "No! I want Rick to come." Tears began rolling down her little cheeks.

Rick patted her back. "It's okay, sweetie. I'll come see you."

"No!" she wailed, clinging so tight to him that his face grew a little purple.

This was worse than she expected. Kylee had gotten too attached to him, as she had feared. And now she had to pry her daughter off the movie star. She reached out to take Kylee but Rick shook his head. "Just give me a minute," he said.

He took her out of the room and Tara could hear Kylee's wails as they went down the hall, then down the steps. Tara rubbed the back of her neck. Why did she do this again? She'd made a terrible mistake. It wasn't worth getting Kylee emotionally attached to another man who would just leave her.

Tara leaned down and picked up the Jenga blocks, feeling like the worst mother in the world. She'd put herself above the needs of her child. She should have continued to clean toilets, paying off her debt slowly like the rest of America.

And now her daughter would be devastated. Kind of like she was feeling right now. Tara fit the lid on the container. How could she walk away from her feelings? From Rick? Why did he have to turn out to be the perfect man for her? She didn't even realize she was crying until a tear fell on her shirt.

She wiped at her cheeks. How had things gotten so messed up? It was supposed to be simple. At least, it was when Rick explained it. Marry for the publicity. Spend a few outings together so the public could take photos. The rest of the time they were supposed to live happily separate lives. But that hadn't happened. She'd gotten all wrapped up in him.

She loved him. Tara brushed a strand of hair away from her face and stood. She placed the Jenga blocks in the box with the rest of Kylee's toys and lifted it. She went outside and put it in the trunk of the rental car Rick had gotten for her. The money was already in her account, but Rick had insisted on paying for the car. Why, she didn't understand, but she went with it. Every little bit of savings would help her and Kylee.

After putting the trash bag of clothes in the trunk, she was ready to head out with Kylee. No need to prolong things anymore. She went inside to search for Rick. His voice carried out of his office. She walked in to see Rick sitting in his office chair, Kylee on his lap. He had the swimsuit issue of *Sports Illustrated* open on her lap.

Kylee looked up. "Rick's reading to me."

Tara raised her eyebrows. "He is? What is he reading?"

"Stories about the swimming princesses."

She coughed to cover up a laugh. "I see."

Rick shrugged. "I didn't have any kid's books."

Tara reached out for Kylee and she climbed into her arms willingly. She took it as a sign. Time to go now, before Tara or Kylee had another meltdown. "We're all packed."

Rick stood up so fast his chair bumped into the wall behind him. "Wait. I got her calmed down, but I think it would be best if you stay for another week or two."

Stay? What would be the point of that? To fuse the bond between him and Kylee even more? "I don't think that's a good idea," she said.

"Why not? What would it hurt? You have a room here. You have everything here."

Tara's throat grew tight. She tried to draw in a breath but it seemed impossible. How could she stay? What would she do? Live in his mansion . . . as what? They were already starting the divorce process. She forced the words out. "I can't."

She turned and walked through the house, Rick following after her. As she neared the front door, Rick ran ahead and opened it for her. He frowned as she put Kylee in the car. He stopped her from shutting the car door. "Stay. Please."

His words stabbed through her. She looked into his eyes, which seemed to hold something unsaid. She wasn't sure why he wanted her to stay longer, and in her heart she knew it would only prolong the inevitable. She needed to move on. She broke his gaze. "I'm sorry. I have to go."

He stepped back, slowly nodding. "Alright."

She climbed into the driver's seat and started the engine. It took all her willpower not to turn around and glance at Rick as she drove away.

***

Rick watched Tara's car wind its way down the driveway, his heart going with it. The summer sun beat down on his skin. Why couldn't he have just said how he felt? How could he have let her go?

His mind flashed back to Scarlett, and pain shot through his chest. He'd let her go, too. Was he that shallow? Could he give up Tara for his life in L.A.? Was she just a hamburger to him, or did his love for her run deeper?

He walked back into his house. He immediately felt the emptiness she'd left. Kylee's peals of laughter . . . Tara's soft perfume. Gone.

He couldn't convince her to stay. Did he have the courage to go with her? He let the questions simmer in his mind as he walked back into his office. He plopped down in his chair and stared at the carpet.

Over the past few days, he'd almost come out and told her he wanted to try to make a real relationship work. But he hadn't been able to gather up the courage. He knew she had her heart set on going to Iowa to raise Kylee. He'd already probed to see if she'd stay. The answer was clear: no.

The only thing he could do was walk away from his career to be with her. But would he turn bitter if he did that? Resent her for what he gave up?

He exhaled and looked up at the ceiling. He missed her already. No, missed was an understatement. He ached for her. The best eight hours of his life was when she'd spent the night in his arms. If he could have that every night, he'd be happier than he'd been his whole life.

A realization slammed into him. He wasn't letting her go for selfish reasons. He was letting her go because he knew she wouldn't be happy in L.A. And he wanted her to be happy.

The situation was totally different with Scarlett. He let her go because he wanted himself to be happy. She was the hamburger. Tara was more than that.

But was she worth more than his career? He picked up the *Sports Illustrated* magazine. Kylee and Tara filled a hole in his life he never knew existed. A hole that now sat empty, leaving part of him dead. Yes, he could give up his acting career to have them in his life. He'd enjoyed his time in the limelight, but he realized now that life wasn't full. It was missing something.

He stood and a yellow form on his desk caught his eye. Kylee's Winnie the Pooh bear. He picked up the stuffed animal and looked at the ratty fur.

Kylee would be heartbroken when she realized she left it.

And he would be heartbroken if they left him.

He grabbed his keys and ran to the garage. Tossing the bear onto the passenger seat, he climbed into his Jaguar and cranked the engine. The garage door seemed to take forever to lift. He peeled out of the garage in reverse, ignoring the smell of hot rubber on concrete.

He flung it into drive and took off down the hill. As he neared the gate, which was open, Tara's rental car came into view and he slammed on his brakes. What was she doing just sitting there?

He got out of his car and ran up to her window. "What happened? Are you okay?"

She rolled down her window, and he could see she'd been crying.

"What's wrong?" he demanded.

She wiped at her face. "Nothing." She gave him a sheepish grin.

His heart pounded, trying to make sense of everything. "Why are you sitting here?"

She shook her head and clenched the steering wheel, looking out the windshield at the palm trees. "I seem to be having trouble leaving."

Rick stared at her, not understanding. "You don't want to leave?" Did he dare hope?

A moment ticked by before she blushed. "I'm sorry. I'm being silly. I should go." She put the car into drive.

He opened her car door. "Get out."

She looked up at him. "What?"

"Get out," he said, his voice lower. His palms grew sweaty. If she was having trouble leaving, maybe he had a chance with her. Maybe he could talk her into staying and trying things out. "Please."

She put the car into park and unbuckled, then awkwardly climbed out of the car, her door open and making a dinging noise. Now that they were face-to-face, he wasn't sure what to say. How could he let her know how he felt about her?

Before he could think about it, he cupped her face and pressed his lips to hers. She closed her eyes, and the kiss turned more passionate. She smelled of vanilla and almond, and he couldn't get enough of her. Heat enveloped him as he wrapped his arms around her.

He kissed her jaw, and then her neck. She let out a soft moan. He pulled back. "I don't want you to go."

She pulled away from him. "But Kylee and I . . . we need to start our life."

"Your life is here. Stay with me." He looked into her eyes and gathered up his courage. "I want to give this a shot."

Chapter 25

Tara wasn't sure she heard Rick right.

"Give what a shot?"

"Us." His eyes held vulnerability. Uncertainty.

She swallowed hard. "There is no us," she whispered.

He ran a finger down her jaw, causing all kinds of havoc inside her. "Don't you feel it? It can't be just me."

"Of course, but a life together can't be built on chemistry."

He frowned. "What I feel is more than that." His gaze flicked to Kylee sitting in the backseat. He turned back to Tara, his gaze penetrating through her. "I've been fighting it, but I can't anymore. When you drove off, I thought I would never see you again. That I'd never get a chance to tell you how I really feel. Tara, I'm in love with you."

Tara's pulse raced. He loved her? Her knees felt weak, and she didn't know what to say. Had her dreams really come true? Rick felt the same way she did?

Sweat formed on Rick's forehead. "If you don't say something soon, I'm going to go crazy."

Elation filled her, and she laughed, wrapping her arms around his waist. "I'm so happy to hear that, because I've fallen in love with you, too."

Relief flooded his face and he kissed her again, this time more leisurely. Tingles erupted through her. He pressed closer until she was backed up against the car, his hands on either side of her. The feel of his muscles against her made her light-headed. When he finally pulled back, she smiled at him. "Have I ever told you you're a really good kisser?"

He chuckled. "Can't say that you have."

"Dang. Remind me to do that."

He ran his fingers up her arm. "I will."

It was hard to concentrate with the way he was making her feel. "Rick?"

"What?"

"Has your attorney filed the divorce papers yet?"

His gaze traveled to her lips. "No."

"Good."

His lips twitched. "Why?"

"Because I think I'm going to enjoy being married to you."

A slow smile spread across his face. "I'll tell him to chuck the papers."

Kylee kicked her feet. "I want to get out."

"Okay, just a minute." Tara pointed to the open door, still making a dinging noise. "I'd better drive this thing back up the hill."

"I'll follow you," Rick said.

***

When they were back up the driveway, Rick grabbed Kylee's Winnie the Pooh and ran to get her out of the car. When Kylee saw the bear, she held out her hands for it. "Pooh bear."

Rick picked her up and held her close. She wrapped her little arms around his neck. He'd almost lost her. Almost lost the feeling of belonging to something bigger. Of mattering to someone so small. He'd never mattered to anyone before. The feeling was indescribable.

He opened the trunk on the rental car and pulled out Tara's garbage bag of clothes and brought them inside. Tara came in with the box of Kylee's toys.

"I need to go talk to my attorney," Rick said.

Tara nodded. "Go." She reached for Kylee, but the little girl clung to Rick and shook her head.

He laughed. "No worries, this Ladybug can come with me."

Kylee giggled at the nickname he'd taken to calling her. "I'm a little girl," she informed him.

"I know, Ladybug."

More giggles.

Rick called his attorney and told him not to start on the divorce papers. "We've had a change of heart," was all he said.

Nerves filled him as he walked back into the other room. Were he and Tara really going to stay married? Was this thing for real? He could hardly believe it.

Tara approached him in the great room. "I asked Eliza to make us something special for dinner. I hope that's okay."

He raised one eyebrow. "Since when are you okay with Eliza waiting on you?"

Tara made a face. "I'm not, but if I'm going to live here, I have to adapt to the way things are done. I don't want Eliza losing her job, or being upset with me for displacing her."

"Wait, you don't want to move to Iowa? I thought you had your mind set on it."

Tara stared at him. "I thought . . . I mean, I thought you were asking me to stay."

"Stay with me. Stay married. If Iowa is where your heart is, I'll go there with you."

Tara blinked. "You would do that?"

Kylee wiggled and he set her down. Rick pulled Tara to him. "I already chose my career over love once. I don't want to do it again."

Tara laid her head on his chest. "I don't want you to move to Iowa. I want to stay here, but it means a lot to me that you were willing to go."

He kissed the top of her head, emotion flooding through him. "I thought you hated L.A."

She smiled up at him. "It's grown on me."

"Really?"

"You've grown on me, really. And I know how much you love L.A."

He hugged her. "There are some nice things here. Things to do."

She pulled back from him. "There's only one thing I want to do right now."

"What's that?"

She brushed her lips over his in a feather-light kiss. "Be with you."

Epilogue

ara resisted the urge to shield her face from the camera flashes. She should be used to them by now, but for some reason, it still seemed surreal. Rick tucked her under his arm and grinned at her. The flashes went off with more intensity. He patted her baby bump. Now that it was too large to hide, the press was going wild.

"When is your baby due, Rick?"

"Is it a boy or a girl?"

"What's your next movie?"

Rick put up his hand and gave them all a stellar smile. "No more questions, please. Thank you, folks. We'll be heading inside now."

He held the door for her to the restaurant. The smell of freshly baked bread teased her nose as she entered. The restaurant was dimly lit, flickering candles on the tables. The walls were covered in deep red wallpaper. They were seated at a quiet table in a secluded area. Rick pulled out his menu, still grinning.

"You love that, don't you?" she asked.

"What?" He couldn't stop grinning.

"All the attention. You're just glowing."

He chuckled. "No, you're the one who's glowing."

She ran her finger along the edge of her menu. "There's a lot to celebrate tonight."

He reached across the table and took her hand. "I'm so proud of you getting into graduate school. You're going to rock it."

"Thanks," she said. "I'm proud of you, too. Sounds like this remake of *Rear Window* is going to be a big deal."

"The cast is amazing. They're pulling out some big names for it. I think it should do well."

She nodded. When the story came out that they had actually fallen in love through their fake marriage, and after they stayed married, they became Hollywood sweethearts. The public loved them, and Rick's career took off again.

The waitress stopped at their table. "Would you like something to drink?"

"Just water, thank you," Rick said.

Tara smiled. Rick still had the occasional drink, but he'd put the binging and getting drunk behind him. She knew he had only been using the alcohol to forget Scarlett. Or to cover up his guilt over how they broke up. But together they'd worked through that painful part of his past.

They placed their orders and Rick sat back in his chair, his gaze traveling over her. "I can't believe we've been married for five years."

"Seems like just yesterday when you strutted around me like a peacock, commenting on my nice 'hometown' look."

He laughed, his eyes crinkling in that sexy way. "And you spilled coffee on my lap."

She blushed. "Yeah, that was classic. I'm still amazed you didn't fire me."

"I couldn't have fired you. You were too adorable." His cell phone made a chime and he looked at the screen. "Kylee's asking if she can go to Heather's house tonight."

"Did she finish her chores? When I checked, she was sitting in her room, pouting. If she can't find time to vacuum her floor, she doesn't have time to go to Heather's."

Rick typed into his phone. "You're such a mean mom."

"I know. That's why she's asking *you*." She laughed. "You're a pushover."

He shrugged. "I pay a staff to keep the house clean. It keeps food on their table."

Tara didn't want to get into it with him, not on their anniversary, but she had to stand her ground. "That's fine. We've come to that agreement. But Kylee needs to learn how to do these things for herself, or when she moves out her house will look like . . . well, have you seen *Hoarders*?"

Rick cringed and set his phone down. "Alright, I told her she needed to clean her room before she could go to her friend's house."

Tara picked up her water and took a sip. "Are we all set for my parents' visit next month?"

"Yes, I made all the arrangements. Your father even called me twice to make sure we had it on our calendar."

She shook her head. "He sure has mellowed out."

"I think he started liking me after I hit Bobby in the face."

"I think so too," Tara said, fighting back giggles.

"Speaking of Bobby, is he up for parole this year?"

"No. I think it won't be for another year." She still couldn't believe her ex-husband had filed for bankruptcy, then tried to conceal assets. What an idiot.

The server brought them their food, setting the hot plates in front of them. Tara picked up her fork. "When will filming start?"

"Not for a couple of months." He stabbed a piece of shrimp and stuck it in his mouth. "We'll have time to get the nursery ready."

Tara grinned, thinking of the ultrasound they'd had earlier. "Should we do neutral colors like yellow and green? Or go all masculine?"

"Oh, definitely masculine. My son's not sleeping in a yellow room." He winked at her.

"Then blue it is. I'll do some shopping tomorrow."

After they ate dinner, they climbed back in the limo. Rick told the driver to take them home. He slid his arm around her and she snuggled into his side. "Thank you for coming after me that day. I was considering going back to tell you how I felt, but as I thought about it, I had convinced myself it was stupid. I was about to drive away when you showed up."

Rick kissed the top of her head. "Even if you had driven away, I would have searched until I found you. I wouldn't have lasted a day without you."

She looked up at him. Before she could say anything, his lips were on hers. Somehow, even after five years of marriage, he could still make her insides tingle. She returned the kiss, running a hand through his hair.

He tugged the fastener out of her hair and it spilled down over her shoulders. She smiled, ruining the kiss.

"What?"

"You never did like my hair up."

"It's a little triumph for me when I can pull it down."

She laughed. "I love you."

He nuzzled her neck, kissing along her collarbone. "I love you too."

Tara closed her eyes, basking in the feeling of Rick's kisses. How did she end up so lucky? She was truly amazed that she had everything she ever wanted. She just hadn't known she wanted Rick Shade.

The End

ABOUT THE AUTHOR

Victorine lives in Nebraska with her husband, four children, and two cats. She loves all things romance, and watches *While You Were Sleeping* about once every six months. When she's not writing, she's designing book covers for authors, or making something in her craft room.

Join Victorine's mailing list and get a free Kindle book at www.victorinelieske.com.

Other books by Victorine:

Married Series:
Accidentally Married
Reluctantly Married
Mistakenly Married
Blissfully Married
Acting Married

Romantic Suspense:
Not What She Seems

Paranormal Romance:
Falling for the Beast

Young Adult:
Isabella and the Slipper

Science Fiction:
The Overtaking

If you have enjoyed Acting Married, please leave a review. As an indie author, word of mouth is so important. Tell your friends you enjoyed this book!

In case you're wondering what's coming up next for me, here's a sneak peek of Isabella and the Slipper, coming out soon!

Isabella and the Slipper

Chapter 1

The school gymnasium bustled with excitement. Isabella winced as a brawny guy crammed onto the bleacher, practically sitting on top of her. He smelled of locker-room sweat, and Isabella grunted as the air squished out of her lungs.

Her best friend, Savannah, turned to glare at him. "Hello? Someone's sitting there."

The guy cast Isabella a blank stare. "Sorry," he mumbled, scooting over a millimeter.

"Maybe look next time before you sit?" Savannah said to him, rolling her eyes.

"Won't do any good. I'm invisible, remember?" Isabella pulled her phone out of her pocket and sighed. That was the story of her life.

Savannah moved over to give her room and snatched the phone from Isabella's grasp. "Let me see your new phone."

The cheerleaders ran onto the gym floor, shouting and waving their pom-poms.

Ugh. There was so much to hate about mandatory pep rallies.

"You have no fun apps." Savannah nudged her. She had her hair up in pigtails, and she looked like she had just stepped out of an '80s magazine with her sparkly lips and denim jacket. "You haven't even put your name in here."

"I just got it last night."

"You'd better put a password in, at least. What if someone steals your phone?"

"Who'd do that?" Isabella wanted to laugh but saw that Savannah was serious. "I'll do it tonight."

Savannah slapped it back into Isabella's hand. "At least you have a cool case."

"I know, right? The Beatles were legendary." She pocketed her phone. The cheerleaders were forming a pyramid, and she didn't want to miss it if one of them toppled off.

"I'm still surprised your stepmom let you get a phone."

"I think it's because she wants to be able to hound me even when I'm not home. She's acting like I owe her big-time now. Never mind that Delilah and Ava have had phones since middle school."

Savannah smirked. "If I were you, I'd have run away a long time ago. Your stepmom is the worst."

Isabella didn't want to get into it. She was holding out, waiting for graduation.

Just one more year and she'd be gone. Not even Savannah knew how horrible it was living there, in her father's house, but not belonging. Unloved and unwanted.

She pushed her glasses up her nose. "You said it."

A deep voice rang out over the speakers, and Isabella's heart involuntarily sped up. Chase Hawkins. The most popular guy in school. *And* an actor. Who could forget the roles he'd had in two major Hollywood movies? Not leading roles, smaller stuff, but still. He was a movie star, and the whole school treated him accordingly.

Chase was her stepsister's dream man. Isabella had to hear about him every morning as Delilah rushed about, getting ready for school. It made her want to throw up. It might be because Isabella didn't want to admit to herself that Chase affected her in much the same way as every other female in the school. Especially in physics—he sat right in front of her, and she had to smell his heavenly cologne all period long.

"Are we ready for the game tonight?" he shouted, and the crowd burst into a screaming frenzy. Chase walked to the center of the gym floor with a wireless microphone. "I can't hear you!"

Isabella feigned boredom but couldn't help staring at Chase. His dark hair was never perfectly styled, yet it fit his easygoing manner. His smile made her toes curl, and his blue eyes were sigh-worthy. He handled being in front of the crowd with ease. It was in his nature.

"All week we've been collecting change for our 'Kiss the Pig' contest." Cheers rang out, and he waited for everyone to settle down again. "I'm sure you've seen the teachers' jars all over the school." More cheers. "It's time to announce the teacher who collected the most change and has to kiss the pig."

Screaming erupted, and Isabella held in a smile. Even though the pep rallies weren't her thing, she couldn't deny wanting to see a teacher kiss a pig.

Jason Scott, the quarterback, came out of the locker room wearing his football gear and carrying a squirming pig. It squealed its disapproval at being manhandled. The crowd went nuts, standing and stomping, making whatever noise it could.

Chase pulled an envelope from his pocket. "In this envelope is the name of the teacher who won."

There was no settling the crowd down now. Even Savannah was screaming. Isabella stood, pulled her phone out, and turned on the camera.

There would be perks to having a cell phone.

She focused in on Chase, zooming in so his face filled the screen. No one heard the click of the shutter on the app—they were too busy hollering.

"Do you want to know who it is?" Chase asked, eating up the attention.

Isabella figured she would probably be deaf after this pep rally.

Chase opened the envelope and tugged the piece of paper out. He grinned and pulled the microphone close to his lips. The gym grew quiet. "Mr. Morgan!" he shouted.

The pig squealed as if in protest, and the entire school blew up. Savannah jumped up and down, shrieking. Brawny guy scowled at her.

Mr. Morgan taught Isabella's physics class, and he was probably the coolest teacher in the school. He had actively campaigned for his jar to get the most change. All the students loved him; he was young and energetic.

The gym exploded again as Mr. Morgan ran onto the gym floor waving at the bleachers.

Jason held up the pig, and Chase tried to calm everyone down. "Let's give the man a little silence, please."

Mr. Morgan put on a show, waving his hand in front of his face like the pig stank. Then he walked around, pretending to contemplate where he should kiss the pig, pausing and looking close at the back end. Laughter rose from the crowd. Isabella snapped another photo, this time of the pig and Mr. Morgan. When he finally leaned down and kissed the pig on the top of its head, cheers erupted and Chase whistled.

"Come to the game tonight and watch us kiss East Ridge High goodbye!" Chase waved one arm, signaling that the students could go.

The cheerleaders stood at the doors handing out candy kisses to everyone. Isabella waited until the mad dash for the doors had dwindled into more of a solid throng before starting down the stairs. "I wish you could come to the game tonight!" Savannah yelled over the noise.

Isabella held in a snort. "Delilah would die if I showed up at a game. I'd ruin her social status or something. I'd rather avoid the drama."

Savannah gave her a pitying frown and hugged her. "See you Monday."

Isabella nodded and gave her friend a little wave. Her weekend would be spent running the art gallery her father, Anthony Shepherd, had established before he died. Her stepmother, Mrs. Elenore Shepherd, was too stately to do something as lowly as man a gallery. That fell to Isabella's shoulders.

She pulled out her phone and fiddled with the photo she'd shot of Chase. She'd caught him while he was smiling, showing his perfect white teeth and a small dimple in his cheek. It was a good shot. She stepped onto the gym floor.

"The pig is loose!" someone screamed.

In an instant, the gym turned into a mass of running students. Some tried to catch the pig while others tried to avoid it. The pig ran past her legs, squealing with what she could only imagine was glee.

"There it is!" someone shouted.

A cheerleader slammed into her and Isabella's phone went flying. Her heart lodged in her throat. Not her new phone!

It clattered to the floor about two yards from her. She prayed no one would step on it and crack the screen before she reached it. She pushed her way through the crowd, trying to not lose sight of the phone. The pig ran past her again. Someone kicked her phone, and it skittered across the gym.

Her heart pounded. She couldn't see it. *Please, no.* She couldn't lose her phone on the first day of having it! She fought against the steady stream of kids, trying to see where it had landed. *There!* She saw it. It was on the floor near the wall. She focused on it and shoved her way through.

Just before she could grasp her phone, a hand reached down and picked it up. "Hey, that's mine!" she said, as she looked up to see . . .

No. Not him. Anyone but him.

Chase grinned at her, holding out her phone— and another one with an identical Beatles case. "Hey, look. We have the same phone case."

"You like The Beatles?" she asked, then mentally rolled her eyes.

Brilliant. That was a completely idiotic thing to say.

He grinned. "Who doesn't?" But he wasn't looking at her anymore. His gaze ran beyond her.

She turned to see Mr. Morgan holding the pig. "Got him!" he shouted. Everyone cheered.

She grabbed her phone from his hand, but Chase didn't seem to notice.

"See ya at the game." He brushed past her and ran to catch up to Jason, who slapped him once on the back before they disappeared into the crowd.

And that was it. Her first conversation with Chase, and he didn't even really look at her. She was upstaged by a pig.

***

Chase jogged across the parking lot to his Mustang convertible. He unlocked the doors with his key fob and slung his backpack onto the seat.

Friday at last. Football and fun with the guys. This weekend was going to rock.

He climbed into his car, clicked the button to put the top down, and started the engine.

Delilah Shepherd came running across the parking lot in her ridiculously high heels.

"Chase!" she shrieked, waving her hand. She was Barbie blonde and had about as much empty space in her head as the doll.

He held in an eyeroll. He was just too nice. That's what it was. He didn't have the heart to tell her he wasn't interested. "Hi, Delilah," he said as she stopped, panting.

She grinned at him and adjusted her purse. "Some of the guys are coming to my house later tonight for a small get-together after the game. I thought maybe you'd like to come."

Delilah's parties were always popular. Most of his friends were probably going to be there. "Sure. Sounds fun."

Her grin spread, and she placed her hand on his arm. "Great. I'll see you tonight."

She took off, and he could see her younger sister waiting for her by their car. They giggled and jumped up and down before getting in their red sports car and driving off. He shook his head.

See? Too nice.

He threw his car into drive and skidded out of the parking lot. Even with Delilah after him, he knew he would still have fun that night.

His phone made a noise. What kind of noise was that? When he stopped at the light, he checked it. There was a text, but he didn't recognize the number. He looked closer at the phone. It looked brand new. The tiny crack in the corner was gone, and there were no scratches on the screen.

Dang, he had the wrong phone.

He pulled off to the side of the road and read the message.

Where are you? You're late. If you don't show up immediately your precious phone privileges will be gone.

Ouch. The girl from the gym was in trouble, and she didn't even know it.

He swiped the phone open and touched the messaging icon. He typed in his phone number.

We accidentally switched phones. I think your parents are texting you asking where you are.

He waited a minute before realizing she didn't have a way to answer back; his phone was locked. He sent another text.

Unlock my phone. 110900

A message came through.

Oh my gosh, your phone will not stop beeping at me. I don't even know what Snapchat is. You've got so many messages. Sorry about the phone switch.

That's OK. Your mom sounds angry. You better hurry home. We can switch phones back tonight at the game.

He slid the phone into his cupholder and pulled into traffic. Five minutes later, he parked in his driveway. The phone beeped again, and he picked it up.

I'm not going to the game. We'll have to switch them later. Sorry.

She wouldn't be at the game? Who was this girl? Didn't the whole school go to the games?

He tried to remember what the girl looked like, but he couldn't think of her face. Did she have brown hair? Blonde? He wasn't sure. She was shorter than he was, and that's all he remembered. He texted her back.

Who are you?

He figured he could look her up in the yearbook so he'd know who he was talking to. As he waited for her answer, he climbed out of his car and grabbed his backpack. Walking into the house, he checked the screen, but no more texts had come through.

Huh.

His mother met him in the kitchen, her dark hair set up in electric curlers. "Excellent. You're home. I can tell you the good news."

He inwardly groaned, but didn't let it reach his throat. "What?"

"You have an audition tonight. Quick. Go shower and change. This is a good one."

His mouth dropped. She knew he had plans. Why would she do that?

"Mom, there's a game tonight!" He knew he sounded whiny, but he couldn't help it.

She narrowed her eyes at him and folded her arms. "Then aren't you glad you're not on the team? This is why we decided you shouldn't try out. It's your career we're talking about. Not some unimportant football game."

His heart sank. It wasn't *his* career. He didn't want it. "It's important to me. It's the first game of the season."

She got that look on her face, the one that said he'd better do what she wanted or he'd be in trouble. "It's one audition. They are making special arrangements for you to come in tonight. Don't sass me about it. You can go to the game after."

He let his shoulders fall. There was no point in arguing with her. His father would have his head if he talked back to her. "Okay."

"Go get ready. The script's on your bed. Memorize your lines before we leave."

He nodded and ran up the stairs. His phone beeped, and he swiped to read it.

Your mom texted. Sorry, I was walking and didn't see it right away. She said something about an audition.

He answered her back.

Yeah, I know, I just talked to her. I'm going to miss the game.

Getting an audition is good though.

He snorted.

If only I wanted to be an actor.

He hit "Send"—then instantly regretted it.

Why did he say that?

He didn't talk about that with his friends. They all thought he was cool because he'd had a few roles in the movies. There was a pause, and then another text came.

Why do you do it then?

That was a complicated answer.

Parents.

Oh. Sorry. That stinks. I know how that is.

Who was this girl? He was curious enough to poke around on her phone. He opened her contacts, but they were empty. Didn't she have any friends in her phone? She hadn't even put her name in. Just her number showed at the top of the screen. Weird.

He tossed her phone on his bed and stripped down to his boxers. He turned on the shower to let the water get warm and grabbed a towel out of the closet. A half hour later he was dressed and picked up the script. When he saw what role he was trying out for, he confronted his mother.

"Mom, this is a major part." He flipped through the pages and pages of text. "This isn't something I can do during school."

She smiled. "We'll get you a tutor. Then you wouldn't have to go to school every day. Honey, this is the role we've been waiting for. You're ready for it." Her eyes shone, and she flipped her curly hair behind her shoulder. "Come on, you can memorize in the car."

Just what he wanted.

Not.

Learn more about Isabella and the Slipper at www.victorinelieske.com.